A LITTLE GAME

A LITTLE GAME

by Fielden Farrington

WALKER AND COMPANY

New York

First published in the United States of America in 1968
by Walker and Company, a division of Walker Publish-
ing Company, Inc.

Library of Congress Catalog Card Number: 68–16681.

Published simultaneously in Canada
by The Ryerson Press, Toronto.

Printed in the United States of America.

Book design by Lena Fong Lueg

To Mark

Chapter 1

THE TWO BOYS sat silently side by side in the coach, their pale-blue uniforms serving only to emphasize their dissimilarity. Robert Reagan, who sat nearest the window and looked out of it with a sullenness that was clearly habitual, was spare, tall for his years, which were thirteen, taut, and too adult-looking. Stu Parker sat on the aisle side of the seat, his chubbiness straining his uniform, his round face intent. He was reading a comic book.

Robert stirred in his seat and Stu looked up at him. "You want a comic book? I must have about seven hundred."

Robert turned his head slowly to study Stu. "What would I do with a comic book?"

"Well, read it."

Robert returned to his view from the window. "Comic books are for idiots."

Stu shrugged. "So I'm an idiot. I like comic books." He grinned and settled down to his book once more.

Robert watched the rocky countryside without appearing impressed by it. Up ahead, muted by the coach's insulation, the diesel engine made a low growling sound, and its horn, like a cross between an automobile horn and a fog horn, blew with authority. Robert frowned fleetingly, more likely at some unwelcome thought than at the landscape. His face, handsome but with no show of feeling to warm it, was too pale. His lips were thin, sharply defined, and had a look of potential but unrealized mobility.

The conductor entered at the front of the coach, sliding open the door and closing it behind him expertly without turning. He stood there for a moment, smiling as though pleased with his passengers and swaying comfortably with the coach's motion. "All tickets," he called. "A-a-all tickets." His voice was high and nasal and had an indefinable quality of comedy.

Stu said, "If I don't start thinning out pretty soon, like everybody says I'm supposed to, I'm gonna end up looking just like that."

Robert studied the conductor for a time and then nodded. "And just as stupid, too. Here, give him mine." He handed Stu his ticket.

The conductor worked his way back toward the boys, canceling out tickets and putting narrow strips of cardboard in the backs of seats in return. He had something to say to each passenger, and almost everyone smiled at whatever it was. One small white-haired lady laughed outright and appeared to blush faintly. The conductor winked at her and moved on. His face actually was a good deal like Stu's when he winked.

He came at length to the boys' seat and Stu handed him the two tickets. He looked them over gravely and said, "Well, now, you two must be from Hastings Military Academy. Right?"

Stu nodded. "Yes, sir."

"Good school. I always heard it was a good school." He punched the tickets and stuffed them into a side pocket of his uniform coat. "Expensive but good. You on your way home for the holidays?"

"Yes, sir. Well," Stu amended, "Bob here's on his way home. I'm just going with him to visit. I mean, I'm not going to my house."

"Too far, I expect." The conductor forced two of his narrow cards into a slot in the back of the seat ahead of the boys.

"Well, see, my mom's in Florida this winter, and she figured, you know, what's the sense in me going all the way down there for Christmas. So Bob here asked me to his house."

"That's nice." The conductor beamed at Robert, who looked back at him as if at something alien. He turned quickly to Stu again and said, "That's nice," a second time.

"Sure beats staying at the Academy," Stu said. "All by myself except for a bunch of droopy teachers."

The conductor grinned. "Pretty droopy bunch up there, are they?"

"You can say that again!" Stu leaned forward in his seat and looked up at the conductor earnestly. "We got this guy teaches American History . . ."

"Stu!" Robert made the single syllable incisive enough to silence Stu at once. "Don't keep the man here talking all day. He has work to do."

"Oh. Excuse me," Stu said.

The conductor studied the two of them for a moment, nodded gravely, and moved on.

"Won't you ever learn to keep your big fat mouth shut?" Robert asked Stu quietly.

"For Pete's sake, I wasn't saying anything."

"Nothing but your life story. You'd have been talking about the game next."

"Aw, come on now, Bob."

"Stupid kid." Robert kept looking down at Stu until the chubby boy began to fidget in his seat. "Blabbermouth."

"Now, don't start that again, will you? When did I ever blab about any of . . . I mean, you know, that stuff?"

"Never when I was around, naturally. But how do I know what goes on when my back's turned? How do I know how much you run off at the mouth when you get loose?"

Stu looked hurt. "Well, you could take my word for it. I've told you often enough, haven't I?"

"Have you?" Robert let one corner of his mouth tilt up slightly. "Tell me again."

"Pete's sake, what do you want from me?" Stu said. "I don't blab about, you know, any of that stuff."

Robert took Stu's left arm in a grip that turned his knuckles white. "You know what happens if you do, don't you?"

"Hey, knock it off, will you? That hurts."

"You know what happens?"

"Yeah, yeah, you told me a million times."

Robert relaxed his grip somewhat without releasing Stu. He said, "Are you going to keep your mouth shut when you get to my house?"

"Didn't I tell you!"

"If I catch you spilling anything to my mother or . . . or her husband . . ."

"How often do you want me to say it? I promise."

"You know what will happen."

"Brother! I know, I know."

Robert released Stu's arm and gave him a smile that had something almost paternal in it. "I just hope you won't forget."

Chapter 2

As PAUL AND Elaine walked through the concourse from Lexington Avenue toward the gates in Grand Central Station, he kept snatching quick little looks at the ghostlike reflections they made in the shop windows. It was a foolish thing he often did when he walked with Elaine, feeling, he supposed, a certain pride just in being one of a pair which she completed. He liked to look over her head and see her reflected between himself and the window, tall and straight. She complemented his own six feet and two inches very well, and no reflection was misty enough to hide her beauty from him.

"We ought to hurry, Paul," she said, tilting her head to look up at him. "Their train's due in just a minute or so."

"We'll make it. Who's this kid he's bringing with him?"

"Stu, Robert calls him. Short for Stuart, I imagine. I don't know whether it's a first or last name. Do you think I'll cry when I see Robert?"

"I shouldn't think so," Paul said.

"I don't know. It seems years since he left, and I just . . . I don't know."

If she meant that she had butterflies in her stomach, Paul could match them. It was always an unpleasant time for him when Robert was at home. Elaine drew away from him at these times, behaving like someone he didn't know, some strange woman he had no business living with. Robert seemed to drain the personality out of her. And, in addition, there was always the danger she would simply tire of the disharmony between Robert and himself and ask him to leave her. He knew, he was very certain, that she had been on the point of doing so several times in the past.

They passed an optometrist's shop and the bluish-gray drapes drawn across the window brought their reflections out sharply. He could even see the worry in his face. It was a gaunt face at best, not Lincolnesque exactly, but with more than a hint of that kind of solemnity. His students called him Old Pain-in-the-Face, he knew. He tried to smooth the worry lines out, but they walked past the optometrist's shop and he couldn't be sure he had succeeded.

"I hope it's going to be all right this time," Elaine said.

"What do you mean?"

"You know what I mean. Isn't that what you're thinking about?"

"All right. Yes, that's what I'm thinking about. I'll do the best I can."

"Well . . ." What she meant, he felt sure, was that his best had never been good enough yet. "I just can't understand what's so difficult about it."

Robert is what is so difficult about it, he would have liked to say. Robert and his determination to hate my guts, no matter what. He didn't say it, naturally, but he would have liked to.

The gate was already open, and they could see a diesel engine pulling a long train toward them. The train stopped with a jerk. Robert won't like that, Paul thought. There was a pretty girl in the information booth who kept smiling at him. A student of his, he supposed, or a former student. It embarrassed him. He hoped Elaine wouldn't notice it. He realized that he had a dull headache. Because he was here to meet Robert?

"Is my hair all right?" Elaine asked him. "I'm so excited."

"It looks fine to me."

There were a good many boys in the pale-blue Hastings uniform, but Elaine was able to pick Robert from among them without any trouble at all. "There he is," she squealed. It didn't even sound like the voice he was accustomed to. "The little fat boy with him must be Stuart."

Robert looked taller, Paul thought. Could four months make so much difference? At Robert's age, he supposed they could. He wore his uniform more like a man than the others. He pushed the fat boy along in front of him up the stairway and then left him to hurry toward Elaine. They kissed and people stared, thinking, if their expressions could be trusted, how touching it was. Both Paul and the fat boy stood a little apart, also watching.

Robert turned at last and said, "This is Stu. Stu, this is my mother and that's . . . her husband."

Stu gave Robert a puzzled look and then marched up to Elaine, holding out his hand to be shaken. "My name's Stu Parker. Thank you very much for letting me come home with Bob for over Christmas and everything."

"You're very welcome indeed, Stuart. Is it Stuart? We always enjoy having Robert bring his friends home with him."

Paul tried to remember a time when Robert had ever brought a friend home with him before.

Stu marched up to Paul, reaching for him with his right hand. It turned out to be a sticky hand. "Stu Parker, sir. Thank you very much for letting me come home with Bob for over Christmas and everything."

"We're very glad to have you, Stu," Paul said, and he meant every word of it.

Robert and Elaine sat together in the back seat of the Cadillac.
Stu rode up in front with Paul. Elaine's voice went on and on,
talking to Robert, questioning him, and although Paul couldn't
quite understand what she said, the pitch and inflection of her
voice made him uneasy. The uneasiness felt familiar. Robert and
Elaine were together again.

"Boy, some car!" Stu said. "I bet you could go about a
thousand miles an hour if you wanted to."

"It's pretty fast," Paul told him. "I've never had it over
about eighty, but it's got a lot more in it than that."

"That's for sure."

Stu had an odd smell that Paul had noticed before in the
presence of little boys, and even boys no longer quite as little as
all that. It was a sweetish smell made up of sweat and hair and
probably sheer growth and whatever they had in their pockets.
Robert had never smelled that way. It wasn't exactly perfume, but
Paul enjoyed it.

Although the real rush period was still more than an hour away,
the Queensboro Bridge was already clogged with traffic. Christmas
traffic, of course. It increased the edginess Paul was already
feeling.

"How do you like this bridge, Stu?" Robert said.

Stu peered out the window, twisting in his seat in order to get
a wider view. "I didn't even know we were on a bridge," he said.
"It's too big. It don't even feel like a bridge."

"My father used to build them just as big," Robert said com-
placently. "Bigger, maybe. My real father, you know."

Stu glanced quickly up at Paul and then quickly away again,
embarrassed.

Robert's real father's name had been Stan Reagan, and he must
have been a great man, Paul thought, if only because he had been
able to make Robert—well, and Elaine, face it—believe he was so
great. Paul had never seen him, of course, except in old photo-
graphs, but he envisioned him as the complete swashbuckler:

sometimes the classic engineer standing a little apart on an eminence, shouting and pointing while lesser men scurried about building magnificent bridges and such according to his instruction; sometimes the great hunter stomping through this or that jungle in a safari jacket, killing off the wildlife; and sometimes the great lover. Paul did his best not to overvisualize this last one. Was it possible for a man to give the impression of being so much of so many things without being a phony in at least one or two areas? Paul had never been able to learn, really, what other people had thought of Stan. The neighbors who had known him, former friends of Stan's and Elaine's, all seemed determined not to talk about Stan at all, as if it were some sort of conspiracy. Perhaps that answered his question, Paul thought. Perhaps it was the most eloquent answer he could possibly have been given.

"Hey, they got the houses trimmed for Christmas!" Stu said. "The whole houses. Look, Santa Claus and the reindeers up there! See? On top of that house?"

"Cheap," Robert said.

Paul looked back at Robert quickly. "Depends on your point of view," he said, turning back. "If you're thinking cheap, it's cheap." He wasn't sure Robert and Elaine had heard him.

"I kind of like it," Stu said.

There were millions of boys in the world, Paul reflected, and of them all, of all those millions, Robert was the one he had drawn as a stepson. It was the only possible way, of course, to be married to Elaine, which, in turn, was the only way he could imagine living, but it did seem a high price to pay.

Paul had been aware of Robert's disapproval from the beginning, but he had not recognized it as pure hatred until some months after his marriage to Elaine. It had been a lazy summer Sunday afternoon, and Paul, at loose ends because Elaine was upstairs writing letters, had wandered into the library to find Robert lying on the leather couch reading an extraordinarily large book.

Robert had put his finger in the book to hold his place and sat up slowly. He didn't move like a boy. That was the first odd thing

Paul had noticed about him. All his mannerisms, even his speech habits, were quite adult. He sat up now and said to Paul, "Are you going to be in here long?"

"I don't know. Probably not. Why?"

"Because I'll find someplace else to read if you are."

"No, don't leave because of me. I'm just wandering around." It hadn't been a happy beginning, but Paul could remember thinking, in spite of that, that this might be an opportunity to get on some kind of more acceptable footing with Robert. "Pretty heavy-looking book you're reading there."

"Is that the way you judge books? By the pound?"

"Hardly."

"Oh, that's right; you're a schoolteacher, aren't you?"

"I'm a full professor of English at . . ." He was ashamed at once of having made the distinction. "I'm a schoolteacher, yes."

"I always forget." Robert checked the page number and put the book aside. "Mother keeps telling me, but I always forget." He brushed his hair back with his fingers, although it didn't seem to need brushing. "What did you do in the war? You must have been in one of them. I can't imagine what a schoolteacher would do in a war."

"I was on the staff of *Stars and Stripes* for a while."

"Oh." Robert smiled. "My father was a Marine. And he built bridges." He waved a relaxed hand to show Paul the wall covered with books. "These are mostly about bridges and dams and things like that. I've read quite a few of them. I'll read them all, sooner or later."

"You're interested in engineering?"

"Not particularly. I'm interested in my father." The contempt in Robert's eyes shocked Paul. "My father thought all school-teachers were fools. 'Those that can't do it teach it.' That's what he used to say. You didn't come in here looking for a book, did you?"

"No, I didn't. And as for——"

"Because we don't like outsiders messing around with the books."

"I don't think you can call me exactly an outsider," Paul said quietly.

"That's what I call you. I don't know what Mother calls you, but I call you an outsider."

Paul realized that he must either accept defeat or do something physical to the boy, and that this, in the long run, would constitute an even more severe defeat. He turned to leave the library.

"Oh, another thing . . ." Robert said and left it hanging.

Paul turned back. "Another thing?"

"You've noticed the gun rack, I guess."

Paul nodded. One of the things he disliked most about the room was the glass-fronted case on the back wall near the outside door. There were six guns in it, four that Paul took to be rifles and two shotguns. He didn't really know that much about guns.

"They were my father's," Robert went on. "He was a hunter, my father was. Not just rabbits and ducks, but . . ." He sighed deeply but allowed nothing emotional to reach his face. "Anyway, I wouldn't advise you to fool around with the guns, either. They might be loaded, you know. Don't fool around with them."

Later on, Paul had tried to talk to Elaine about this, but she simply hadn't seemed to understand what was wrong with it.

They came to the sharp corner where Grace Avenue turned into Shore Road. As Paul eased the car around the turn, Robert said to Stu, "It's not far now. You'll like the house. My father was the architect. It's a very good house, isn't it, Mother?"

"Yes, it is." Elaine said it quite distinctly.

Stu stirred restlessly on the seat, bumping Paul's arm with his shoulder. He seemed to feel that there were too many fathers here. It was making him uncomfortable.

The house stood on a gentle rise, so that they could see its roof from some distance. Then the Cadillac made a wide left turn, and the whole house was there like a fanfare. It stood on an acre and a half, and all the trees were behind it. An extravagant sweep of

unshaded lawn rose like an ocean swell from the road to the front
of the house. The grass had turned brown now except for small
patches of greenish resistance, but since the lawn's distinction de-
rived more from contour than color, it was impressive all the same.
There were four thick, white, two-story-tall pillars in front of the
house, supporting the roof of a narrow, perfectly useless porch.
The house itself was covered with white clapboards, each a foot
wide, and roofed over with slate. The wooded area behind the
house, rather pretentiously called the grove, grew on a downward
slope and so was very nearly invisible from the road.

Stu said, "Wowee!"

Paul turned the long car carefully into the driveway and, at
almost the same instant, Laura came through the front door and
stood on the narrow porch waiting for them. Laura, the one full-
time servant, was congenitally underprivileged. No amount of
feeding would fatten her up; no amount of good fortune could
shake her gloomy attitudes. She stood at the edge of the porch,
her coat wrapped tightly around her, and waited, shivering, Paul
was sure.

Robert climbed out of the car first and waited beside the door
to help his mother. She put her hand on his arm, stepped out, and
said, "Why, thank you, Robert."

"You two go ahead," Paul said. "Stu and I will get the luggage
out of the car."

With a curious expression, Stu watched them walk away. As
soon as they were out of earshot he said, "Bob was real glad to see
his mother, wasn't he?"

"I guess he was, yes." Paul opened the car's trunk. "I'll hand
these things out to you. Okay?"

"Sure, Mr. . . . uh . . ."

"Hamilton."

"Gee, I'm sorry, Mr. Hamilton. See, Bob's name's Reagan, and
I know your name's not Reagan, but I just . . . I just forgot."

Paul smiled down at him and decided that he was a nice kid and
wondered what he was doing here with Robert. "It's all right. To

tell you the truth, I'm not sure I remember your last name either. Is it Palmer?"

"Parker," Stu said, grinning.

Paul handed out first Robert's two leather bags and then Stu's larger plastic one. "What have you got in here, boy? This thing weighs a ton."

"Comic books," Stu said solemnly. "About a million, I guess. Bob says I'm a stupid jerk because I read comic books, but . . ." He shrugged.

Paul nodded, because he knew what the shrug meant.

They carried the luggage toward the house, Stu insisting on struggling with his own, while Paul took Robert's. Robert was saying to Laura, ". . . glad you're still with us. I was afraid you'd just disappear into thin air or something while I was away."

Laura shook her head and said, "No," with too much breath.

"Laura," Elaine said, "this is Mr. Stuart, Mr. Robert's friend who's come to spend the holidays with us."

Robert chuckled. "Anybody ever call you Stuart before, Stu?"

Stu marched to the porch, tugging at his right glove to get it off. He reached up to shake hands with Laura. She hesitated a little and then took the hand. Her body dipped—she probably meant it for a curtsy—and she mumbled something. Stu marched back to stand beside Paul.

"You can take their things up, Laura," Elaine said. "Put Mr. Stuart's bag in the guest room."

Stu said, "Hey, I get a room all to myself!" Then he looked embarrassed. "I mean, you know, at the Academy, we don't get . . ." His voice trailed off.

"You didn't think I was going to let you bring that suitcase full of comic books into my room, did you?" Robert said, but he smiled. "Mother, don't you think I ought to help Laura with those heavy bags?"

Laura said, "No!" It was not loud, but it was pitched as high as a scream and had something of a scream's quality. "No, I mean . . . two trips! I can do it!" She pounced on Robert's two bags, and almost tripping in her haste, turned and ran for the doorway. "I'll be right back down for the other one."

"It was a nice thought, all the same, Robert," Elaine said. "A very gentlemanly thought."

Chapter **3**

ROBERT LOADED THE last of the rifles and put it back in the glass case. He had cleaned them all and loaded them all—the four rifles and the two shotguns—and he seemed to feel better, now that it was done.

"How come you do that?" Stu asked him. "I mean, why do you have to have them all loaded and everything?"

Robert said, "Do you see this room? Take a look around this room."

Stu had already taken a look, and it had chilled him a little. It was the library, opening directly off the living room. Everything was dark and heavy, and although there were plenty of windows and a door with a glass panel, the light didn't seem to brighten the room. There was light enough to see by, but it had a peculiarly dismal quality. Stu looked around again obediently.

"This room," Robert said, "was my father's. Everything in it was his. The books were his, the couch and the chairs were his, the desk was his, the guns were his. Everything. This is where I come to remember my father."

Stu stirred uncomfortably on the couch, wondering if he ought to be sitting on it. "So did your father keep all the guns loaded all the time and everything?"

"I don't know." Robert looked distressed. "I can't remember. They take a lot of looking after if you're going to keep them

loaded, so maybe he didn't. I do, just in case. When I'm at home,
I do."

"What for, though?"

"Because a loaded gun is a handy thing to have around. Don't
you even know that a loaded gun is a handy thing to have
around?"

The tree dominated the living room not only by towering over
everything else in it but also by out-glittering even the fire. Paul
sat alone, dividing his attention between the tree and the portrait
over the fireplace. The boys were upstairs changing or unpacking,
and Elaine was making mysterious housekeeping talk with Laura
back in the kitchen.

The painting over the mantel was quite large, too large for the
room, really. A man named Ostiner had done it just eight years
ago. As a matter of fact, it had been Stan's last Christmas gift to
Elaine, but Paul was able to forgive it this because he liked it so
much. It was a full-length portrait of Elaine, perhaps one-third
life size, and it was the most beautiful thing Paul had ever seen.
Whether or not it was great art Paul could not say, although Stan
was said to have paid a great deal of money for it. It was Elaine;
that was the point. It *was* Elaine. She stood before this same fireplace, one outstretched hand reaching up to the mantel, her head
tilted back just a little, her eyes focused upon a point high on the
opposite wall. She seemed no older today than when the portrait
had been painted. Paul thought that Ostiner, since he had been a
stranger to Elaine, must have been extraordinarily perceptive, for
the relaxation, the serenity, seemed to spring more from Elaine's
personality than from the outward aspects of her. All the same, he
had caught those outward aspects, too. It was clear that she was
quite tall and that she was well made, without buxomness. She
was just thin enough to have a willowy quality, but not thin
enough, fortunately, to feel breakable to his hands and arms. Her
hair was blond—a little darker now, perhaps, than in the portrait.
She was very beautiful, both in and out of the painting.

"It's a pretty tree this year, isn't it?" Elaine was standing in the wide opening, smiling at him. She had the look, somehow, of having been there for quite a while. "I think I have too many red bulbs over on the fireplace side, but I can fix that later."

"A very pretty tree," Paul said. "Second-prettiest thing in the room. Third-prettiest, actually, if you're coming in."

"Silly." She came in. "Not that I mind."

"How about a drink? It's the day before the day before Christmas, isn't it?"

Elaine laughed. "And only eight more drinking days before New Year's Eve. Is it eight days?"

"Close enough."

"I've already asked Laura to bring a tray in."

Except perhaps for the dressing room upstairs that Paul had turned into a study, the living room was the best room in the house. With Elaine sitting just on the other side of the fireplace, as now, it definitely was the best. It had been redecorated since Stan's death, and it had Elaine's stamp on it clearly. Paul might not have chosen quite the same drapes or such a neutrally colored carpet, but the thing was, Elaine *had* chosen them, and because she had, they went beyond their intrinsic value to partake of Elaine's own worth to Paul. Now he had a good fire going, and it put transient highlights on the mahogany surfaces, gave life to the quiet carpet, and played tricks with Elaine's face.

Laura came in carrying a tray of Scotch, soda, and ice in her bony hands. She put the tray down on the mahogany bureau which served as a bar when one was needed. She said, "Will dinner in about an hour be all right, Mrs. Hamilton?"

"That will be fine, Laura, yes."

The Scotch was twelve years old and quite expensive. Paul couldn't help considering this as he poured it. Their standard of living sometimes strained a college professor's income a little. Some of the money, of course, was Elaine's, formerly Stan's; Paul tried to think about this as little as possible. He was constantly grateful for the semiannual royalties on his textbooks. "Did I tell you?" he said to Elaine. "I talked to old Mosely at Ashley-

Greene the other day. There's a good chance SMU will use the new book next fall."

"How nice."

A lot nicer than that, Paul thought. Of course, Elaine didn't understand how it worked at all.

She said, "Haven't you made mine too strong?" She held her glass up and tried to judge it by its color. "It looks terribly strong."

"Very light, both of them." He sat down in the matching chair on what was traditionally his side of the fireplace. He lifted his glass toward her. "Merry Christmas."

She sipped and said, "You're right; it's fine."

It took him back, almost with a jolt. Things did that to him quite often. It took him back to the day he had met Elaine. It had happened at a cocktail party given by Gerry Luntz, who was Paul's friend as well as his lawyer. Paul hadn't wanted to go, really, but Gerry had been very firm about it—had he perhaps had Elaine in mind?—because, he had insisted, Paul needed to get out more. He had been right, of course. Nadine had divorced Paul only a few months earlier, and he had been feeling pretty sorry for himself.

Gerry had introduced him to Elaine and left the two of them more or less alone together in the crowded room. Elaine had been wearing a tiny black hat with some black feathers—he didn't know why he remembered that so clearly—and she was the most beautiful woman he had ever seen. She smelled very faintly of a perfume that he felt must surely have been distilled from some very delicate pale-blue flower that not many people knew about. Her dress clung to her in such a way as to stir something in him that had not been stirring much at all lately.

"May I get a drink for you?" he asked her. She didn't have one. "You have to carry a glass around, you know. At least."

"Well, I can't drink martinis, and the man who's serving the Scotch makes the drinks so strong they're almost as bad."

"Does he, now?" Paul said. "Why don't we go and have a talk with him?"

In the end, against the better judgment of the caterer's bartender, Paul had mixed Elaine's Scotch and soda himself. "It's just right," she had told him, and it had seemed to him the most significant compliment he had ever received.

She had had dinner with him later at a small place she herself had chosen—Paul had wondered since if it had been her own favorite or formerly Stan's—and then he had driven her home and got his first look at the house on Shore Road in Great Neck. It had given him a shock. Why would she live in such a house if she were unmarried? He couldn't remember whether Gerry had said "Miss" or "Mrs."

Elaine, apparently reading his mind, said, "We were living here when my husband died, and I've just stayed on. My son is strongly attached to the place."

"Oh. Your son."

"Yes. Robert. He's ten years old."

Paul wondered now what he would have done if he had known at the time what that name Robert would come to mean to him. The same thing, probably. Almost certainly the same thing.

Elaine sipped her drink and smiled at him, and he was suddenly flooded with affection for her. He made a distinction between affection and love. They coexisted, he thought, as complementary but sharply individual entities. Sometimes one, sometimes the other, assumed the ascendancy. When affection had his attention, Paul was aware mainly of a great warmth that made him want to grin, even chuckle. He *liked* Elaine. He said, "I enjoy being here with you like this."

"Oh, yes, I enjoy being with you, too." She said it solemnly. "If only . . ."

"No! No if onlies!"

"Oh, Paul, why does it have to be this way?"

And there went the evening. There, maybe, went the whole damn holiday season. A slow anger began to grow, crowding the affection Paul had been feeling. "Drink your drink," he said. "If that's the best you can do, don't talk."

"But we can't just ignore it. We have to talk about it."

Suddenly Paul was fully angry. "All right, let's do that. Let's talk about it." The tenderness wasn't washed out at all; it was simply overruled by anger and distress. "Only, for once, let's make it a two-way conversation. Shall we try that?"

"I don't know what you mean."

"Let's not just hear what you think. For once, let's take a look at it from my angle. I mean, let's *consider* it from my angle, not just throw it out because it doesn't match what you're determined to believe."

"Paul!"

"Well, damn it, Elaine, isn't that what we've always done before? Isn't it?"

Elaine was angry, too, now. Despite the play of the firelight, Paul could see her heightened color. She sat very straight, unnaturally composed from head to toe. She was so beautiful and so thoroughly *Elaine* that it would have been easy for him to capitulate, as he had done too often in the past.

Instead, he said, "Before there's any hope of straightening this mess out, you have to listen to me, Elaine. You have to face the possibility that what I say is true. That's all I ask, for right now. Just face the bare possibility."

Elaine waited a moment and then said, "Well, go ahead. You want to talk. Talk."

"The first thing you have to realize is that Robert is not just one simple person. He is not just the nice boy he lets you see. When you're not around, he can be . . ."

"Now, wait just a minute. If you . . ."

"I haven't finished!" He shouted it.

"All right."

He took a deep breath, needing, more than the oxygen, a second to collect his thoughts. "It's possible for a bright child—and I never said Robert wasn't bright—it's possible for a bright child to appear to be something he's not. Something he just plain isn't by nature. Let me finish. To you, because that's the way he behaves in your presence, Robert is a sweet, loving son, attentive, considerate, a real gem of a boy."

"If that's meant to be sarcasm . . ."

"No, no, just listen to me. If you could know, if you could only know how he hates me! My God, he could kill me. I've seen murder in his eyes more than once, and——"

"Paul, I won't listen to this!"

"All right, all right. That's an exaggeration. I'm sorry. What I'm trying to say is, there's no way for you to know how he behaves toward me—or anybody else, for that matter—when you're not around. He changes—when you come in a room—he changes, like changing his clothes. When you aren't watching, he can be vicious and——"

"All right!" Elaine stood up. She looked very tall. "All right, that's it. That's quite enough." She picked up a poker and jabbed it at the fire, out of anger and not with any intention of improving the position of the logs. "They'll be down soon."

What chance did a man have, Paul asked himself, when he loved a woman in anger as deeply as any other way?

"All I know is, if I talked to my father the way you talk to him —pow!"

Robert put his pen down and turned to study Stu with an expression in which tolerance was mixed with something less attractive. "I keep telling you, Stu, he's not my father. Do you think I'd have talked to my own father the way I talk to him?"

"Oh, yeah . . . well . . ."

They were both in Robert's room because Stu had got lonely in the guest room. "It's great," he had said, "just great, only it's so grownup I don't feel like I ought to take my pants off in there." Robert was now wearing a tight pair of pale-tan slacks and a white turtleneck sweater. Stu had put on a dark-blue suit and a maroon tie with widely spaced white stripes. "It's the first time I had dinner with your folks," he had explained to Robert. "You gotta wear a tie the first time you eat at somebody's house." Robert had been writing something in a leatherbound notebook but had not been able to continue with Stu in the room.

"How about that Christmas tree down there!" Stu said. "Man, that's gotta be about a hundred and fifty feet high!"

"In a room with a ten-foot ceiling?"

"Well, you know what I mean."

"That suit's too tight for you."

Stu shook his head, mock sadly. "The suit's okay; I just try to get too much into it, that's all. You know, there must be about a million packages under the tree down there. Are they all for you?"

"Quite a few of them, I imagine. You'll get something."

Stu was embarrassed. "I didn't mean that."

"Shut up!" Robert held up a warning hand and cocked his left ear toward the door. "Listen," he whispered.

"I don't hear anything."

Robert stood up and moved toward the door. He put his right forefinger to his lips and walked on the tips of his toes. He opened the door suddenly and stepped through into the hallway.

"Well, Laura," he said, "snooping again?"

"I just came up to see if you needed anything, you and Mr. Stuart." Laura's voice was high and breathy, tremulous. "It was your mother herself that sent me."

"Come in, Laura," Robert said. "Come on in. I want to talk to you."

"Well, I got a lot to do. I don't think I better . . ."

"I said, come in, Laura."

Robert stepped back from the doorway and Laura entered with almost comic reluctance, her hands fluttering about the collar of her uniform. Her eyes were wide and dark and thoroughly frightened. "I got an awful lot of work to do," she said.

"Well, I expect you'll find the time for it." Robert closed the door and leaned against it in a lounging attitude. "Have you been a good girl?"

"I don't know what you mean."

"You don't?" A corner of Robert's mouth twitched, but he didn't quite smile. "What I mean is, have you been talking about me?"

"No."

"Are you sure?"

"I haven't even mentioned your name," Laura said. "I swear, I never once said so much as 'Mr. Robert' from the time you left to go to school until a while ago when you came in. Not once, and that's the truth."

"I'll just bet it is."

"Well, all I can do is tell you the truth." Laura looked behind her nervously at Stu. "I got no witnesses."

Robert pushed himself away from the closed door and came toward her. He was tall enough to look down at her, and this seemed to give him pleasure. She shrank back a single step, and his hand moved forward quickly to imprison her arm. His fingers sank into her flesh as if it were indeed made of dough, as it seemed to be. "I wouldn't believe you even if you had a dozen witnesses."

"Please, Mr. Robert, you're hurting my arm."

"I know." He pulled her a little toward him. "Do you remember what I told you I'd do if you talked to anybody? To my mother or her husband?"

"You think I'd forget something like that?"

"I think you'd better not." He released her arm and nearsightedly examined the palm of the hand that had held it, as if to determine whether it had been soiled. "I'm going to be here until the end of next week, you know. You'd better be on your good behavior."

"Can I go now, Mr. Robert?" Laura asked.

"Why not?" Robert stepped back, leaving the way to the door clear. "And don't snoop any more, do you hear? They may tell you to snoop, but don't do it. It's very unhealthy."

Laura reached the door in two of her long, ungainly strides, opened it, stumbled through, and closed it as quietly as she could without wasting time. Robert laughed.

"Man, you were rough on her," Stu said. "What's up, anyway? Is she in on . . . you know, that other stuff?"

"No," Robert said. He sat down at his desk again, all the laughter gone out of his face. "No, that was strictly personal. She's a lousy snoop. Listen." He turned toward Stu and seemed to rearrange his face consciously so that it showed a half smile. "I'm trying to write something here, and I don't see how I'm ever going to finish it if you . . ."

"Hey, you writing in the diary?"

Robert nodded.

"Something . . . you know?"

Robert said, "Maybe."

"You mean, we're gonna keep the game up and all that while we're here? Cripes, I didn't even bring my diary with me or anything. I figured . . ."

"I can get you some paper and a pencil," Robert said.

"Yeah, but . . . well, okay. I just figured, you know, we'd take some time off."

"No rest for the wicked. That's just a corny old saying, Stu; it doesn't mean anything. Listen, why don't you go back to your room and read a comic book or something for about ten minutes? I want to get this finished before dinner."

"Oh. Okay." At the door Stu turned and looked the room over. "You got a real swell room here, Bob. I mean, you know, the stereo and everything."

"See you later," Robert said.

Stu closed the door softly and stood for a time in the hallway, not really wanting to go back into the guest room. What he would have liked to do was go downstairs and look at the Christmas tree some more. It was the most beautiful tree he had ever seen, he was sure, with all the lights and the little cradles and candles and bells that actually rang when you touched them and the tinsel all hanging down perfectly straight, every strand, like silvery rain. The only thing was, if he went down there and found Mr. and Mrs. Hamilton in the room, he was going to be embarrassed. "Well, what the heck," he half whispered to himself. "I'm a guest, ain't I? You have a guest around Christmastime, don't you expect them to look at the tree?"

He crept down the stairway with his hand on the banister, ready to hurry back upstairs if it looked like the best thing to do. He couldn't hear a sound from the living room, which was off the downstairs hallway, through a wide opening to his left. The house didn't look as big, he thought, from the inside as from the outside. The rooms were plenty big and there seemed to be enough of them, but from outside the house had almost scared him. He peeped through the opening into the living room.

Mrs. Hamilton was sitting in one of the big armchairs that faced the fireplace diagonally. She seemed to be staring into the fire. Mr. Hamilton was standing with his back to the fire, looking straight at Stu. Stu said, "Oh!"

"Come in," Mr. Hamilton said, sounding as if he really meant it. "Come on in, Stu."

Mrs. Hamilton twisted around to look at him and said, "Yes, of course, do come in." She tried to see behind him. "Isn't Robert with you?"

"He had some stuff to do up in his room." Stu stepped through the opening. "I just thought I'd come on down and look at the tree some more. That's the best tree I ever saw. I saw the one in front of the RCA Building once, but this is the best one I ever did see anyplace."

"Well, thank you, Stuart," Mrs. Hamilton said. It made him feel strange when she called him that. "What is it Robert's doing up in his room?"

"Oh . . . writing in his diary and stuff."

"His diary!" Mrs. Hamilton was surprised. "Robert keeps a diary!"

Oh, boy! Like Bob said, he was a good kid, but a blabbermouth. "Well, yeah, kind of. Sort of like a diary."

"What does that mean, Stuart? Sort of like a diary? I don't understand."

"Well, just, you know, the stuff that happens to kids. Like, 'Today Rolly Herbert got two demerits' and 'Day after tomorrow Christmas leave starts,' and, you know, junk like that."

"Surely Robert wouldn't keep a diary with nothing but that in it."

"I don't read Bob's diary, Mrs. Hamilton." What the heck did she think he was, anyway? "I don't know what's in it."

Paul stood in front of the fireplace, although the backs of his legs were getting uncomfortably warm now, watching Stu squirm.

Why was it, he wondered, that men—including boys, who had the seeds of manhood in them—would give up almost anything of value to them to avoid unpleasantness, while women seemed to spend their lifetimes seeking it out? He was not, he argued for and against himself, trying to make a case against women; he was simply curious. To a considerable extent involved, too, to be honest.

Elaine had got Stu all the way into the room now and they were sitting side by side on the couch. Stu seemed to have escaped from the diary inquisition, which had made him surprisingly uncomfortable, but he was clearly in for more.

"And are you and Robert roommates?" Elaine was asking.

"No, ma'am. Bob hasn't got a roommate."

"Oh? Isn't that a little odd?"

Stu moved forward on the couch, trying to make his feet reach the floor. "Well, see, he had a roommate, a kid named Johnny Spence, but Johnny . . . well, he had to leave the Academy."

"I should have thought you'd have wanted to move in with Robert right then."

"Well . . . yeah. We talked about it some. But, see, I always have comic books and like that scattered around all over everywhere, and anyway . . . well, I don't know. Bob's kind of different from other kids."

Elaine pounced. "Different? How do you mean, different?"

"Gee, I don't know exactly." Stu looked around at Paul, as if for help. "He just, you know, likes to be by himself a lot. Like he didn't *need* other kids. You know what I mean?"

Elaine leaned back, satisfied. "Yes, of course."

If the boy really had been looking to him for help, Paul decided, he ought to do what he could. He said, "You have football there at the Academy, don't you?"

"Yeah!" Stu beamed at him. "We won three games this year." A shadow crossed his face. "Of course, we lost eight."

"Well, you can't win them all." Paul crossed to the couch and sat down at the empty end of it, with Stu between him and Elaine. The seat of his pants was hot enough to hurt, and he would have liked to stand up again, but he decided against it. "Any new talent coming up next year?"

Stu grinned. "I'm going out next year. I mean, a record of three and eight, I can't do much damage, can I?"

"You've got the build for it." Paul grinned back at Stu. "All you have to do is make sure you lean the right way."

Elaine said, with a high, disturbed quality in her voice, "Robert isn't thinking of playing football, is he?"

"I don't think so, no, ma'am," Stu told her. "He don't like stuff like football and basketball and like that too much. He's pretty good at tennis, though." He added this last as if to atone for the derogatory character of what had preceded it.

"Yes." Elaine was satisfied again.

"Bob talks about hunting too, but we don't get much chance. No chance at all."

Paul felt he had to say, "I'm not much in favor of hunting, anyway. Taking lives. I like the games better."

"Yeah. Well, we got plenty of games at Hastings."

"Games?" Robert's voice from the hallway opening had an almost sepulchral quality. "At Hastings?"

Stu bounced off the couch. For some reason, he looked terrified. "Oh, well . . . we were just talking about football and, you know, like that. That's the only game we even mentioned. Right, Mr. Hamilton?"

Paul nodded. Why should one thirteen-year-old boy be terrified of another? And still be his friend? It was unnatural. Robert crossed the room to his mother, stood looking down at her lovingly for a moment, and then bent forward—how like a man he was!— and kissed her forehead. The terror was still plain in Stu's face. What was it about games? Paul wondered.

Elaine said, "We're having Laura's good veal cutlets for dinner, Robert. Is that all right?"

"Great!" Robert was still smiling, but he kept glancing at Stu. "I always liked Laura's good veal cutlets."

"And tomorrow the regular Christmas Eve dinner. Remember?"

"Spare ribs and baked beans? How could I forget?"

"In here by the fireplace, if you like."

"Yes, I'd like that." And Robert added, speaking to Stu, "We always have spare ribs and a pot of baked beans on Christmas Eve. Laura serves them in here. You can even sit on the floor if you want to. It's sort of a game, you might say."

"Listen, Bob, I didn't . . ."

"We always enjoy it."

From the doorway, Laura made her attention-getting noise, which still sounded to Paul like a whimper, although he knew it was a cough. "Dinner is served now," she said. She stepped aside to let them go out into the hallway and across to the dining room.

Elaine and Robert went first, Elaine's hand on the boy's arm. Stu followed them, but Laura stepped forward, blocking Paul's way. He said, "Is there something you want, Laura?"

"Yes," she whispered. "I have to talk to you, Mr. Hamilton. I just *have* to."

"Well . . . but this isn't a very good time, is it?"

"Oh, not now! Later. Maybe when Mr. Robert goes out, for some reason. I'll be on the lookout for a good time."

"Why can't you talk with Robert in the house, Laura? I don't see any sense in———"

"Because I'm scared, Mr. Hamilton. I'm scared of my life!"

Chapter 4

AFTER DINNER ELAINE and Robert sat close together on the couch, talking softly, sharing secrets, apparently. Paul was left to talk to Stu, which would have been perfectly all right except that Stu seemed to have lost the power—or at least the desire—to speak. He had been frightened and miserable all through dinner. He had eaten, for a fat boy, almost nothing at all.

"Mrs. Hamilton and I trimmed the tree last night," Paul said to him. "Didn't finish until nearly three o'clock this morning." Stu smiled unconvincingly. "Did you ever see such a pile of gifts as that? Christmas is a very big time around here." Stu looked at the packages under the tree obediently and said nothing. "Where do you usually spend Christmas?" A pause and then, "You have to answer direct questions, Stu. It's impolite not to."

"Excuse me," Stu said. "I've always been at some kind of a boarding school or something. Ever since I can remember, pretty near. Mostly, I just stay at the school over Christmas."

Paul touched the boy's shoulder lightly. "That's pretty rough. Are your . . . don't you have any parents?"

"Oh, sure. My father's in Greece or somewhere this winter. He takes pictures for something; I don't know what. My mother spends the winters in Florida mostly. There's no sense in making that long trip down to Florida just for Christmas, is there?"

"I guess not. Anyway, I'm glad we were able to get you out of Hastings this year."

"Yeah," Stu said, "it sure is nice here."

He didn't look as though he were enjoying it much, though, Paul thought. Since the thing about games before dinner, he had behaved like a different boy altogether, and Paul wondered why. He had an intuition amounting to conviction that he was going to have to find out why.

"Stu," Robert called from across the room, "want to listen to some records?"

"Yeah, okay," Stu said. He didn't sound enthusiastic enough.

Robert stood up. He was holding Elaine's hand. "You don't mind, do you, Mother?" he said. "I promised Stu earlier I'd play some records for him. He's crazy about my stereo setup. I don't like to break a promise."

"Of course you don't."

She released his hand, and he kissed her forehead again. Paul told himself that there was nothing wrong with a boy loving his mother or a mother loving her son. If it were another mother and son, he told himself sternly, he would consider it very touching. But it wasn't. It was Robert and Elaine.

Stu stood up and said, "Excuse me, sir?"

Paul smiled and nodded.

Elaine let them get halfway up the stairs before she called, "Oh, Robert?"

"Yes?"

"There's something I wanted to ask you about. Stuart, you go on up to the room. Robert will be right up."

"Yes, ma'am."

Stu plodded on upstairs, his behind wagging like a fat woman's. Elaine had gone to the foot of the stairway, and Robert came slowly back down toward her. He gave her a very brief quizzical look and then turned it into the son-to-mother smile. Paul found he couldn't watch.

"Yes, Mother?" Robert said.

"I have something very serious I want to speak to you about, Robert."

The smile faded. "All right."

"This Christmas—over the holidays, I mean —I want you to try very hard to make friends with . . . with Paul. It isn't just a silly whim, you know, or anything like that. I love both you and Paul very much. You know that, Robert, don't you?"

Robert nodded solemnly.

"And it causes me the greatest unhappiness—the deepest kind of unhappiness—to see the two of you at each other's throats the way you always are. I can't do a thing about it myself, you see. All I can do is just plead with you. You and Paul. Will you try?"

"Well, of course," Robert said. "It's what I've always wanted."

"It means a great deal to me."

Robert looked gravely at Paul, who was still sitting in his chair near the fireplace. He touched his mother's cheek. *"I'll* certainly try," he said.

Robert went upstairs, and Elaine came back into the living room. Paul didn't speak to her. She sat down in the chair across the fireplace from him before she said, "You heard him. It's what he's always wanted."

"I heard what he told you," Paul said softly, as if half hoping she wouldn't hear. "I'm afraid I don't place much confidence in what he says to you."

"I suppose I should have expected that."

They sat for a long while without speaking, Elaine staring into the fire, Paul staring at the second page of his newspaper but not even trying to read it. The silence very soon became unbearable to Paul, and he knew that he was going to have to say something before long, and he knew that whatever he said would be the wrong thing.

Before he gave in to the need to speak, however, both he and Elaine were submerged in an ocean of sound which came roaring down the stairs from Robert's room. It was made up of guitars and voices, thousands of each, from the sound of it, and it rocked the house. It was the new teenage kind of music that Paul didn't understand and couldn't abide, but nobody had ever made the music he would have liked, coming at him with such violence as this.

Elaine said, "Mercy!" and put her hands up to her ears.

"That has to be stopped," Paul said, not at all sure that she could hear him.

She nodded. "Go up and tell them."

"Me? You want me to go?"

"Why not?" Elaine took her hands away from her ears. "Why not?"

"Well, if you don't know . . ."

"Oh, for heaven's sake!" Elaine stood up. "If you're afraid of them, I'll go myself."

"Afraid!" The anger swelled inside him, as violent as the music outside. "Sit down! I said, *sit down!*"

Elaine sank back into her chair, looking puzzled. "Well, all I said was——"

"I heard what you said. And don't try to tell me you didn't know what you were saying. Now, you sit right where you are and I'll go upstairs and take care of this. One way or another."

"Oh, no!" Elaine half rose from her chair again. "If that's the way you feel——"

"God damn it, sit down!"

"Paul!"

"I'm sorry."

He went out into the hall and up the stairway two steps at a time, the music hurting his ears and his anger waxing proportionately. He strode down the length of the hallway to Robert's door and raised his closed fist to knock just as the music ended. He lowered his fist slowly and put his left ear against the door, eavesdropping.

In Robert's room, the two boys sat on the floor exactly halfway between the stereo system's two speakers. Robert had grasped Stu's right shoulder with his left hand, sinking his fingers in painfully. Stu was holding his hands over his ears.

"What was it about games?" Robert asked. He managed somehow to make his voice heard above the noise the music made without shouting. "I mean, what was it really?"

"Turn it down, will you?" Stu said. "I can't hear a thing you're saying."

"Take your hands down from your ears." With his right hand, Robert knocked down Stu's arms. "Now, what was all that about games, down there in the living room?"

Stu shook his head. "Nothing," he shouted. "Just football and like that."

"You were shooting off your mouth."

"I wasn't, I wasn't. Look, your father asked me about the football team, and——"

"I haven't got a father!"

"And I told him we had one. What do you want me to do when they ask me about the football team? Tell me that, will you? What do you want me to do?"

"I want you to swear the oath."

"Aw, come on, Bob."

The music ended and the silence was a physical vacancy, an absence with a positive quality.

Robert tightened his grip on Stu's shoulder. "I said, I want to hear the oath."

"Okay, okay, cut it out, will you? That hurts."

"Well?"

"May I turn blue and my fingers and toes drop off, may everybody hate me and girls laugh at me, may my father get castrated in an auto accident . . ."

"Go on."

Stu finished in a rush. "May my mother get cancer if I ever tell anybody."

"Tell anybody what?"

"You know what."

"You have to say it."

"If I ever tell anybody that you killed Johnny Spence."

Chapter 5

PAUL STOOD OUTSIDE the door to Robert's room for quite a long while, simply because he lacked the initiative to go anywhere else. He seemed to have been turned off. The words, "You killed Johnny Spence," were sharp in his mind, as though he were still hearing them, but they would not translate into a specific intelligence. They were a series of sounds only, horror-producing, but as yet not properly decoded. He left the door and went slowly down the stairs, more to escape from the words than for any other reason.

The living room was unchanged, and Elaine was still sitting in the same chair, and Paul wondered how this could be. She said, "You didn't have to make them stop the music altogether."

"I didn't."

He sat down in his chair, noticing, as if it mattered, that the fire was dying down. He picked up his newspaper, but he found that he could not even bring himself to pretend to be reading it. He folded it neatly and put it down on his lap. "Elaine."

"Yes?"

"How often does Robert have a checkup? With a doctor, I mean."

"Every six months or so. He's always been perfectly well. Paul, is anything wrong?"

"No, no, of course not."

"Paul?"

Paul moved restlessly in his chair, and the newspaper slipped off his lap. "Nothing a doctor would find. That kind of doctor."

"Now, what does that mean?"

"Have you ever . . . oh, never mind."

"Paul, stop that!"

"All right." He knew he wasn't going to tell her the whole thing, though. She was going to have to know sooner or later what he had heard through Robert's door—every word of it, word by word—but he didn't have the courage or whatever it took to tell her now. He didn't know what it was going to do to her. Something pretty damaging, he imagined. If she believed it. If anybody could ever get her to believe it. "Have you ever thought of taking Robert to a psychiatrist?" he asked her.

She looked at him for a time with her mouth actually drooping open, a very un-Elaine-like expression. He braced himself against the storm that was coming, wishing it could have been avoided. And then she laughed. Somehow, it made him angry.

"It's hardly a laughing matter," he said. "That boy needs help. I mean, he needs it now, and he needs it badly."

"Oh, Paul." Elaine was still gasping, still half laughing. "I've never heard anything so ridiculous in all my life. Robert on a psychiatrist's couch! Oh, Paul, can't you see how absurd it is?"

"All right," he said. "All right, forget it." He leaned forward and picked up his newspaper, making it rattle. "Just forget all about it."

"If I've ever known anybody in my life who *didn't* need analysis, it's Robert. Paul, whatever put such a preposterous notion into your head?"

"I said, forget it." He opened the newspaper at random to a page of editorials. There were pictures of some of the writers, and they all looked troubled. You think you've got troubles? he asked them silently. You think you've got problems? He kept on repeating it in his mind until he had to stop himself with an effort of will. What did you do when you heard what amounted to a confession of murder from your own stepson? Did you go rushing to the police? When the boy's mother was Elaine and you loved her? What did you do?

Elaine said, not laughing now, "Paul, did something happen while you were upstairs talking to the boys?"

"I didn't talk to them."

"But you went upstairs expressly to . . ."

"The music stopped, and I didn't bother them."

"Oh."

In paperback novels and movies and television plays, people hired private detectives when, for one reason or another, they were unable to take their troubles to the police. Were there really such people in the world as private detectives? Paul had never met one. And what could a private detective do for him, anyway? Well, he supposed, find out definitely if a boy by the name of Johnny Spence had died an unnatural death, if *somebody* had killed him. That would do something for him, wouldn't it? Bring him a step closer to whatever it was he had to do? He folded his newspaper and put it on his lap again. "Elaine, I think I'll have to go to the city sometime tomorrow."

"Tomorrow! The day before Christmas? Paul, the traffic will be impossible!"

"Yes, I expect so. But I've just remembered something I have to talk to old Mosely about."

"Mosely?"

"At Ashley-Greene. They're the people who are bringing out the new book, you know."

"Oh. Yes, of course. It can't wait, I suppose?"

"No, I'm afraid not." It had waited too long already, Paul thought. Too long for Johnny Spence. If there was any truth in it. "No, it's something I have to take care of right away."

"What a shame!" The honest regret in Elaine's face, regret for his inconvenience, made him somehow feel guilty. Of what, he couldn't think. She sighed and said, "Well, I suppose if you must, you must. Will you want the Cadillac or the station wagon?"

"It doesn't matter."

"I guess I'd better keep the wagon here. The day before Christmas and everything, you never know what you might have to haul."

"All right."

"Oh." She frowned for a moment in thought. "Maybe you could do something for me."

"In the city? Sure."

"Two things, actually." She made a careless little laugh which Paul didn't altogether trust, because it was so careless it suggested calculation. "All I got for Stuart was that silly little box of ties, and Robert's going to have so many things."

Paul nodded. "I'll get him something."

"I've noticed he doesn't wear a wristwatch."

"All right. And the other thing?"

"Well—wouldn't you know?—Robert says there's only one thing in all the world he really wants for Christmas, and of course it has to be something I didn't get for him."

"What is it?"

"Maybe you could pick one up for him while you're in the city. I don't know. Abercrombie and Fitch, I suppose, or someplace like that. Men know so much more about these things."

He waited for her silently.

"Paul . . . he wants a rifle."

"A what!"

"Oh, you needn't worry. He knows how to use a rifle. His father taught him all about them."

Chapter 6

THE CITY STREETS were crowded like a cocktail party. The gaiety of the season, which appeared to make the crush bearable, even enjoyable, to the others, had deserted Paul completely last night. He was here on an errand grim enough to have turned the season grim.

He had no need to see Mosely at Ashley-Greene, of course. He had lied to Elaine about that, a thing that stuck uncomfortably in his conscience. He had bought a watch for Stu at a small jewelry shop on Third Avenue, near the garage where he had left the car. A watch that counted days and months, as well as minutes and hours, had tempted him until he was told its price. Then he had settled for a simpler instrument, expensive enough, at that, which rewound itself, could be submerged in water without damage, and was practically indestructible, according to the jeweler. He did not look for a rifle. He and Elaine had settled that, rather unpleasantly, last night.

He found a drugstore at the corner of Forty-eighth and Third Avenue with two phone booths. He went into one of them, dropped his dime in the slot, and dialed Gerry Luntz's number.

"Merry Christmas," Gerry said. "You're not in the city, are you?"

"Yes," Paul told him. "There's something special I had to come in for."

"It's a mess, isn't it? What's on your mind?"

"Well . . . I wondered if you could give me the name of a good reliable private detective."

There was a little pause. "Detective?"

"Yes. I've got something I think I have to . . . to see a private detective about."

"Want to tell me about it?" Another short pause. "Listen, Paul, people don't start looking for private detectives until there's some kind of trouble. I'm your lawyer, don't forget, and people start looking for lawyers when they're in trouble, too. Or ought to."

"It's a personal thing, Gerry. I hope you understand."

"Elaine?"

"No, no, nothing like that. Nothing in the least like that."

"Well . . . okay. Hold on a minute." While he was waiting, Paul considered telling Gerry the whole story. It didn't seem a very good idea. Gerry was a good friend, but also, as an attorney, a sort of officer of the court. He had heard that expression somewhere. Paul didn't want the law involved, at least not yet, even at second hand. "Paul? This is a fellow I use sometimes. Good man, honest and dependable. Got a pencil? Al Dunlap at Crown Investigations. Got that down?" Paul scribbled it on the back of an envelope and added the Lexington Avenue address and the telephone number. "It's a pretty scruffy-looking office," Gerry finished, "but don't let that fool you. Dunlap's a good man. And Paul?"

"Yes?"

"If he advises you to see me, you come and see me."

"Yes. I'll remember that. And thank you very much, Gerry." Paul held the telephone's fork down for a moment and then dropped in another dime and dialed the detective's number.

"Crown Investigations," a woman's voice said. It was a very well-bred voice, and this somehow threw Paul off stride.

"My name is Paul Hamilton. I'd like to speak to Mr. Dunlap."

"Do you wish to engage our services?"

"I want to talk to Mr. Dunlap about it," Paul told her. "I don't know what I want to do until I've talked to him. Mr. Luntz advised me to get in touch with Mr. Dunlap. Mr. Gerald Luntz."

"Oh, yes. All right, when would you like an appointment?"

"Well . . ." He hadn't thought about making an appointment in advance. "I'm at Forty-eighth and Third Avenue right now. I expect it's an imposition, but I'd like to see Mr. Dunlap right away if it's possible. I could be over there in five or ten minutes."

"I see. Just a moment." After a muffled conversation—she held her hand over the phone's mouthpiece, Paul could tell—she said, "Mr. Dunlap will arrange to see you as soon as you can get here, sir."

"Thank you."

Crown Investigations was on the third floor of a sad building which was surely nearing the end of its life span. The reception room was cramped, although utterly bare. Paul could hear somebody invisible using a typewriter. He or she was not very good at it. As he came in, he faced a skimpily varnished partition of plywood with a door that fitted poorly and a square opening through which he could see a girl at a small switchboard. She was quite attractive, what he could see of her, in spite of badly protruding blue eyes. The eyes gave her an extraordinarily alert look.

"Yes, sir?" she said.

"I'm Paul Hamilton," he told her. "I phoned you a moment ago about . . ."

"Yes, of course." She twirled herself about in her swivel chair, and disappearing and reappearing almost at once, pulled the badly fitting door in toward her. "Please come in."

On the other side of the door was a long, narrow room—or a room, rather, which looked long because it was so narrow—with two desks from which the veneer was peeling, both equipped with aging typewriters. At one of them sat the typist Paul had heard, a thin, earnest young man who leaned nearsightedly over the paper upon which he was writing.

"Right through there," the girl said, pointing. At the back of the room were two open doorways. "Mr. Dunlap is expecting you."

A man appeared in the left-hand opening. He was a thick man, so broad in all directions that he appeared squat, although he must have been close to six feet tall. He had a bored face with a mustache that grew too far out beyond the corners of his mouth. The lines at the eyes and from the nose to the mouth were probably premature. His smile seemed forced. "Al Dunlap," he said. His handshake was too firm to be anything but calculated.

"It's good of you to see me on such short notice," Paul said. He wondered if that were the proper tone to take. It sounded social.

"Glad to do it. Come in."

The room was Spartan. The desk was large but it had never been decorative, and it was old now and the top was dappled with circular gray stains. Pushed back from the desk's kneehole was an old swivel chair that listed to the back and right in a way to suggest discouragement. The single chair for visitors was wooden, uncushioned, and stark-looking. On the right wall hung a single document, sealed and signed, which might as easily have been a high-school diploma as anything else.

"Please sit down," Dunlap said.

Paul did and found the chair as hard as it looked.

Dunlap walked around the desk to his own chair. He had a swaying walk because he was slightly bowlegged. He sat down, making the chair cry out, smiled, and waited for Paul.

"To tell you the truth," Paul said, "I don't quite know how to go about this. I've never had any dealings with . . . with a detective."

"We're a good bit like other people. I mean, it's just another business deal. Would a drink help?"

"No, thanks, I don't think so."

Dunlap managed somehow to bring his chair up straight, so that he sat forward with his arms on the desk top. "The chances are," he said, "since you're here at all, that there's something you want me to investigate. So all you have to do is tell me what it is and give me what information you feel I'll have some use for. If I think I need more, I'll ask for it. The whole thing strictly confidential. Okay?"

Paul smiled. "Okay. I'm interested in one of the boys at Hastings Military Academy. Do you know where that is?"

"Hastings." Dunlap frowned. "Westchester County, wouldn't that be? 'Way up there. Other side of Peekskill."

"That's right."

"So, who's the kid?"

"His name is Johnny Spence. That's what the boys call him." After a short pause Dunlap asked, "And what about him?"

"Oh. Well, I don't really know anything about him." Paul worked a cigarette out of his pack and put his lighter to it. His hands felt unsteady. "I've only heard his name mentioned. Johnny Spence. I'm not sure he's still at the Academy, to tell you the truth."

"He doesn't even go to the school, maybe?" Dunlap said. "And that's all you know?"

Paul looked down at the burning end of his cigarette. "I'm not even sure he's still alive."

"Oh." Dunlap took a dark, gnarled cigar from the left-hand top drawer of his desk, bit the end off, removed the tobacco shreds from his mouth almost daintily with a thumb and forefinger, and lit the cigar with the last match out of a crumpled book. His hands were quite steady. He seemed an altogether steady person in spite of the stains on the desk top. "So, what is it you want to know about the kid?" he asked.

"Well . . ." What exactly was it he wanted to know? "If he's alive, just who his parents are and where they live, and where he is now if he's left the Academy."

"And if he's dead?"

"Well, in that case, I'd want to know how he died. From what, you understand? And where. Who signed the certificate and . . . you know more about these things than I do."

"I'm going to tell you the truth, Mr. Hamilton," Dunlap said; "I don't care much for this."

"What do you mean?"

"You don't give a damn about this kid if he's alive, do you?"

"Well . . ." Paul looked about for an ashtray, and Dunlap scooted a battered, unwashed one across the desk toward him. Paul eased the ash off his cigarette with exaggerated care. "All right, I'm not interested in him if he's alive."

"How do you think he died, Mr. Hamilton?"

"That's what I want you to find out for me."

After a moment of thoughtful silence, Dunlap said, "I don't want to get mixed up in anything. I'm not homicide, you know."

"I haven't said anything about homicide."

Dunlap smiled in a way that made his mustache look unevenly trimmed. "I heard you."

"Look," Paul said, "there's no way you could get involved in anything unpleasant. I'm quite sure of that. It's really just my own curiosity that needs satisfying, that's all. I don't mind paying something over your usual fee, but I don't think——"

"That won't be necessary," Dunlap said crisply. "Either we do it or we don't." He sat for a time looking vacantly at the high-school diploma or whatever it was, drawing the corners of his mouth down sharply so that his mustache now turned mandarin. "You don't want me to do anything, right? Just get the facts?"

"I certainly don't want you to do anything."

Dunlap drew a deep breath, and speaking as he released it, said, "Okay. How soon do you need the information?"

"Well, as soon as possible," Paul told him. "Tomorrow is Christmas, of course, so . . ."

"I work holidays." Dunlap was suddenly brisk. "Bound to be somebody out there at the school. Best time, most likely."

"I don't like to spoil your Christmas."

Dunlap shrugged. "I got no family."

"Then, that's very good. How much would you say——"

"I wouldn't. Not until I know what I'm up against. All I can tell you is, you won't get the same quality of work any cheaper anywhere else. Okay?"

"I guess that's fair."

"I'll need fifty now. A hundred might be better. For expenses and like that."

Paul drew the checkbook out of his pocket. The young man had stopped typing in the outer office, and Paul could hear the traffic noise out on Lexington Avenue. It seemed to him that he was too far removed from the everyday world, here in this detective's office, to be within earshot of such an everyday sound. He signed the check, tore it out, and handed it to Dunlap.

Dunlap studied it for a moment, spread it flat on his desk top, and weighted it down with something that looked like an ivory cueball with the bottom flattened out. "One thing," he said softly. "If you think you know something about a homicide, you better go to the police with it. I mean, for your own good, you better. It's nothing to fool around with, homicide isn't. In all fairness, I have to tell you."

"Thank you."

Dunlap took another of his deep breaths. "Okay," he said.

Chapter **7**

DRIVING HOME IN the Christmas Eve traffic, which moved enough to make an accident an easy possibility but not enough to get anybody where he was going, Paul began to think of the thing Robert had done—had *perhaps* done—more and more as a crime, less and less as a boyish prank. Al Dunlap's talk about homicide had done that to him, he supposed. He began to think of Mr. and Mrs.

Spence, Johnny's parents, as people instead of just dimensionless shadows. Probably they loved their son as much, or almost as much, as Elaine loved Robert. He tried to imagine what the loss of Robert would do to Elaine. It was unthinkable. But there were Johnny Spence's parents . . .

He began to worry about Stu. If the Johnny Spence thing were true, then was Stu safe? Was anybody safe, for that matter? Well, Elaine, of course. But Stu was only a boy, and a promising boy. A boy, to tell the truth, whom Paul had begun to like very much. And he was afraid of Robert. He had shown that very clearly last night, at dinner and later.

Paul discovered that he was blowing the Cadillac's horn, holding the chrome ring down. He had no idea how long he had been doing it. He thought that he had better get hold of himself, and while he was thinking it, blew the horn again.

Once on Shore Road, out of traffic at last, he forced the heavy car along the winding lane at a perilous speed. He remembered Stu saying, "I bet you could do a thousand an hour if you really wanted to push." He skidded into the driveway and found the station wagon blocking his way. The simple everydayness of it calmed him down. He was lucky, he reflected, not to have killed himself, driving that way. He had stopped the car, turned off the motor, and was just opening the door to let himself out when he heard the shot. He was quite sure that it was a gunshot. The sound bounced off something and the echo was like a hard slap with an open hand. The shot had seemed to come from the grove, behind the house.

Leaving the Cadillac's door open, Paul ran as fast as he could up the gentle slope toward the house, around the house, and down the matching gentle slope toward the grove. The sky had turned quite threatening, very dark and hanging low over the trees, and Paul thought with outrageous irrelevance that it might turn out to be a white Christmas. There was another shot, sharp and clear and quite unmistakable.

He plunged into the grove, which was not really civilized enough to run through. The underbrush needed cutting away, and he felt it clutching at his trousers. There was a small natural clearing at the far corner of the grove, and Paul headed for that. He thought he saw a movement ahead of him and tried to run faster.

Robert and Stu were standing face to face in the clearing. Robert was holding a rifle, butt downward, against his left foot. Stu was making an impassioned plea of some sort, to which Robert was listening with an indulgent smile. As Paul came close enough to hear, Stu was saying, ". . . and you know it. You said I could if I came out here with you." Then they heard the sound of Paul's running. Stu whirled to face the noise, startled and looking guilty. Robert stood where he was, turning only his head and looking more bored than startled.

Paul pounded to a stop just inside the clearing and stood staring at them, too breathless to speak for a moment. They stared back at him. When he could, Paul said to Stu, "Are you all right?"

"Yes, sir."

"Why shouldn't he be all right?" Robert asked.

Paul said, "Both of you, I meant."

"Why shouldn't we both be all right?"

"I heard shooting."

"Bob shot a tin can off the top of that hedge," Stu said. "From clear back there by that tree."

"What did he promise you?" Paul asked Stu. "What did he say you could do if you came out here with him?"

"Just take a shot at a can or something with the rifle," Stu said. "That's all."

Paul turned to Robert. "Why did you want to bring him out here in the first place?"

"Why did I want to bring him home with me?" Robert said lightly. "We're friends."

Stu looked up at Robert with something like gratitude in his eyes, and Paul felt a wave of frustration. How was it that he saw through Robert so easily and nobody else seemed to? Well, he answered himself, because Robert simply didn't give a damn what he thought. He had some use for the others; he had no use whatever for Paul.

"I want you to take that gun back to the library," Paul said, "and put it back in the case where you got it."

Robert lifted the rifle by its barrel with his left hand and flipped it so that his right hand caught the stock. The right hand inched forward toward the trigger as he turned at last to face Paul. Paul was reminded uncomfortably of the pictures he had seen of GIs in World War II, in Korea, in Vietnam, holding rifles in exactly this way: down low, almost down to the right hip, but infinitely ready. When Robert had come around fully to face Paul, the gun also, as if only by coincidence, was pointing at him.

"Put it back?" Robert said with heavy innocence.

"Now."

From somewhere—probably in the grove; it didn't sound as distant as the house—Elaine's voice called, "Robert?"

Robert looked up at the leaden sky in exasperation and lowered the gun so that it pointed at the leaf mold between himself and Paul.

"Robert?"

"Out here, Mother. In the clearing."

"I thought I heard a gun go off." Elaine appeared from around a clump of yews, looking disturbed. She was wearing a suit which was tweedy but hardly warm enough for this raw December day. "Did you shoot a gun off, Robert?"

Robert looked contrite, and Paul thought it was a pretty outstanding dramatic achievement. "Just for practice," he said. "I'm sorry. I should have told you."

Elaine half smiled at him. "You're not supposed to, anyway, you know. There's a law in Great Neck about shooting off guns."

"Oh. I didn't know that."

Elaine turned to Paul. "I saw you drive in. I hope it wasn't too bad in the city. Robert, please put the gun away, will you?"

"Yes, I was just going to."

Chapter 8

THE TRADITIONAL CHRISTMAS Eve dinner of spare ribs and baked beans—Paul had long suspected that a little investigation would show this to be one of Stan's favorite meals—went surprisingly well. Nobody but Paul appeared ill at ease. For the first time, Stu ate the way Paul had expected him to eat, smearing his face liberally with the fat from the spare ribs. Robert and his mother did most of the talking and kept it light. Stu and Paul grinned at each other from time to time for no real reason at all. Paul was guilty of reflecting that with a little luck he might have had one like Stu for a stepson instead of one like Robert.

When it was over, Elaine nested together the dessert dishes, and holding them safely away from her suit, stood up. "I think I'll take these out," she said. "Would you mind bringing the coffee things, Paul? Laura's so busy out in the kitchen because of tomorrow, I hate to ask her to fetch and carry."

Paul stacked the cups and saucers beside the coffeepot on the black tray, and feeling clumsy, followed Elaine out into the hallway. "It was all right for Laura to fetch and carry up to now," he said to Elaine. "What are you up to?"

"Listen." She came up close to him and spoke in a cloak-and-dagger sort of whisper. "I'm going to take Stuart downstairs to the rumpus room and keep him busy playing Ping-Pong for a while."

"You're what!"

"All right, I want him out of the way. I want him and me both out of the way." She set the dessert dishes down beside the coffee things and took the tray out of Paul's hands. "You go on back in there. I'll come and get Stuart in a minute. You're going to have a talk with Robert."

"Oh, now, wait just a minute! I don't know what you think ——"

"We have to get it settled! You and Robert have got to get it settled! How long do you think we can go on this way?"

"But what good will it do to——"

"That's up to you. You and Robert. There's nothing more I can do; surely you see that."

"But . . . but why tonight?"

"Why not tonight? You'd try to get out of it, no matter when I fixed it. Well, wouldn't you?" She took a backward step and looked up at him with so much distress in her face that his rising anger suddenly died. "I can't take much more," she said. "Not very much more at all."

"All right." He touched her cheek lightly with a forefinger, wanting to show her something he could think of no way to say. "I'll do the best I can."

She turned away from him and went toward the kitchen, walking firmly. There was to be no nonsense about this. He wondered how he was going to justify making a friendly gesture toward Robert and at the same time suspecting him of . . . well, murder. There was no way to justify it, of course. The only thing to do was try to forget the suspicion temporarily, since he had made a promise to Elaine. It would make no difference in the outcome in any case. The outcome was accurately predictable.

He walked back into the living room slowly, trying to prepare himself. Robert and Stu were sitting together on the couch, not moving or saying a word to each other, and this seemed unnatural on Christmas Eve. Or any other time, given two normal thirteen-year-old boys. Paul went to the fireplace and stood for a time looking down into the remaining embers. Then he straightened

and said as brightly as he could, "Well, it'll be Christmas almost
before we know it now."

Stu said, "Yes, sir."

"When I was a boy," Paul went on, "Christmas Eve was the only
night in the year when I went to bed early without making a fuss."
It occurred to him as he was speaking that the only person he knew
before whom he could not help making a fool of himself was
Robert. He could lecture to a bunch of college kids who didn't
give a damn about what he was saying and keep them perfectly
in line. He could make his department head, the president, even
the board of trustees listen to him and take him seriously, important men, men before whom it would not have been unreasonable
to quake a little. He could and did face them squarely and with
confidence. Before Robert, he babbled. "I always thought the
sooner I went to sleep, the sooner the waiting would be over. I
wanted to shut my eyes and open them on Christmas morning."

"Are you trying to get us to go to bed or something?" Robert
asked him.

"Oh, no. No, I was just reminiscing." His smile felt frozen,
assumed like a burlesque queen's. "That's the way you feel on
Christmas Eve when you get a little older. Like reminiscing."

Stu said, as if trying to help, "My father told me he used to try
to stay awake and see if he could catch Santa Claus. I tried it a
couple of times, but I always went to sleep. Little kids can't stay
awake very long at night, I guess."

"When I was five years old," Robert said remotely, "my father
told me that all the Santa Claus talk was just nonsense. He didn't
believe in lying to his own son."

"I guess I'd rather get lied to a little," Stu said.

There was a kind of wisdom in that, Paul thought. Perhaps
that was the basic, the functioning difference between people like
Stu and people like Robert. The one had occasional, maybe very
rare, flashes of wisdom and enjoyed a comfortable mediocrity the
rest of the time. The other was always brilliant but disbelieving,
possessed of a wealth of knowledge, all of which was negative. Of
one thing Paul was quite certain: nobody was going to change

either of them by engaging him in a little talk before the fireplace on Christmas Eve.

From the hallway opening, Elaine said, "Stuart."

Here it comes, Paul thought. Here I stand, frightened of a thirteen-year-old boy. Frightened, God damn it, frightened!

Stu had twisted around on the couch, trying to face Elaine. "Yes, ma'am?"

"Do you like to play Ping-Pong, Stuart?"

"Yeah, sure, Ping Pong's a great game—uh—" Stu glanced quickly at Robert—"game."

"We have a table downstairs in the rumpus room," Elaine said. She was talking to Stu the way she thought children wanted to hear grownups talk, and it was Paul's opinion that children didn't want to hear grownups talk that way at all. "I'll bet I can beat you."

"Well . . ." Stu looked at Robert again.

"Go on," Robert said. "My mother wants to play Ping-Pong with you."

Paul watched Stu cross the living room to the hallway and disappear into it, wagging his behind. A nice kid. And then he realized that he was alone with Robert.

"Well!" he said, and after he had said it could think of nothing to add. He sat on the couch beside Robert and helped himself to a cigarette out of the crystal box on the coffee table. He took his time lighting it, trying to think of something more eloquent than "Well" to say to Robert. That was quite enough for him, and, he felt sure, for Robert too, but it was going to take a good deal more to satisfy Elaine.

Robert said, "Mother's decided we ought to have a little talk. Right?" He lifted one corner of his mouth without really smiling. "Did you tell her how hopeless it is?"

"Well, now," Paul said, sounding stupid to himself. And not in the least sincere. "How do we know it *is* so hopeless?"

"How do we know my name is Robert and yours is Paul?"

"I don't see what's in that to stop us. As a matter of fact, your mother's right; it *is* time we had a talk. We've been going along for two years or better now, sniping at each other and . . . well, you know what I mean."

"Yes, I know what you mean."

"And where has it ever got either of us?" Paul paused for a moment, not for an answer but for a not completely impossible effect. "I don't mind telling you, it's made my life pretty miserable. And your mother's too; that's certain. And I don't see how it can have made you any happier. So what I'd like to suggest is a truce. Not a permanent one, if you think that's impossible, but one at least to last through the holidays. To make the holidays pleasant for your mother." And to allow Al Dunlap time to find out about Johnny Spence. "How about it?"

"What I can't understand," Robert said thoughtfully, "is how she does it. My mother, I mean. How, every so often, she can make you come crawling to me this way."

Paul pointed a forefinger at Robert and stabbed at him with each word. "Now, you listen to me, young man; if you think you're going to take that line with me and get away with it, you can just—" He stopped and slowly lowered the pointing hand to his lap. He took a very deep breath and allowed the air to escape in a long noisy exhalation. "Oh, no." He smiled. "That's your stock in trade, that kind of discussion, and we're not playing this your way. And for your information, this is why I'm here—crawling, if you like to think of it that way: I love your mother very much. I don't know whether you do or not, but I do. I don't intend to lose her."

"We'll see." Robert said it with a kind of calm complacency that made him seem more adult than Paul. "I can wait."

"You have a long wait. I promise you, a very long wait."

Robert shrugged. "I'm young."

It was not like talking to a boy at all. It was like talking to a crafty man, a man whose cleverness sprang from a kind of cynicism that was almost impossible to refute. You defeated yourself in advance if you made any sort of appeal on an emotional level. You had to subdue him with sheer power, Paul realized, and he didn't know where the power was to come from. "No," he said, "you can't win this one."

Robert laughed. It was as unpleasant as any laugh Paul had ever heard. "I think when the time comes to decide—when my mother absolutely has to decide—you'll be the one to go. Yes, I think so. And I'm like my father. I hate compromises."

"I don't think it's going to be that simple," Paul told him. "I don't believe——"

"My father," Robert said, interrupting firmly but with an uncharacteristic softness in his voice, "went to Hastings Military Academy. That's why I'm there, of course. He didn't fool around with football and those things while he was there, but he was the fencing champion. His last year, even the instructor couldn't beat him. He didn't like tennis; he only played because it kept him in shape, and still nobody could beat him. What do you think of that? They couldn't beat him, and he didn't even like the game."

"That has nothing to do with what we're talking about," Paul said, regretting the petulant tone at once.

"Later on, at VMI," Robert continued, as though he had not heard Paul, "he didn't bother with school sports at all. He went off every summer and hunted big game. He killed a wild boar while he was still at VMI."

"Listen to me," Paul said. The boy had simply lifted the talk out of his hands, taken it over. "This is not what we're here to talk about."

"He came back from Korea with a Purple Heart and a Silver Star."

So he was a hero. Paul came very close to saying it; it was a very near thing.

"He had a horse," Robert went on, "a stallion named Geronimo. Nobody could ride him but my father; nobody else could get near him. He boarded the horse at the Wheatley stables on the old estate. Do you know where that is?"

"Listen, Robert——"

"One day—I was watching; I was there—Geronimo stepped in a gopher hole or something. He flipped right over, like a backflip in the air, and landed on my father. Everybody came running, and there was a doctor from somewhere. But do you know what? My father wouldn't let them take him away until he'd shot Geronimo himself. Because of the broken leg. He died that night. My father, I mean."

"All right," Paul said.

"So why would I want you around?"

Chapter 9

PAUL WENT UPSTAIRS to wait for Elaine. He would have a short wait, he was sure. Elaine's timing in matters of this sort was like second sight. He went into the master bedroom and through it to his study, which had begun life as a dressing room. The study was a good little room, except that it was a permanent reminder of Paul's first defeat at Robert's hands. Indirectly, at least, at Robert's hands. Elaine had always thought of it as a compromise, but Paul knew defeat when he saw it. He had wanted to make the library downstairs into an acceptable place for grading papers, writing his textbooks, and all the other work he had to do at home, but Elaine had refused to hear of it because of Robert's attachment to the library just as it was, just as Stan had left it. The argument had been short but bitter. It had left some scars.

The dressing room had been large as a dressing room, but it made a small study. Paul didn't mind that. There was room for a couch that opened up to become a bed when it had to, a deep armchair, and a small but adequate walnut desk. It wasn't very well ventilated and he couldn't type in it after Elaine had gone to bed, but he didn't really mind. It was his own place.

He sat in the armchair now, grateful for the comfort of it. The temptation to close his eyes was strong, but he was determined to resist it. He recognized the weariness he felt as an emotional thing, an outgrowth of this new defeat he had suffered. Defeat, however, was not the same thing as surrender, and he felt that to close his eyes and invite sleep, to try in this way to blot out the ugly fact of defeat, would be to surrender.

From downstairs he heard Stu shout, "Hey, Bob . . ." and something else indistinguishable, which meant that Elaine would be up to talk to him soon. He tried to think of something to say to her. One thing. Just one thing that would not precipitate disaster. There was no such thing, short of outright falsification. "It was a useful talk?" Like the politicians? "A basis has been established for further negotiation?" Like the people on strike? Nonsense.

Elaine came into the bedroom, hesitated a little, and then crossed it to the study door. She stood there for a moment, frowning at Paul, and then entered and closed the door softly. "Well?"

Paul shook his head. He still couldn't think of a single acceptable thing to say.

"What does that mean, sitting there shaking your head? Does that mean you didn't get anywhere?"

"I couldn't . . . yes, that's about the size of it."

Elaine went to the couch and sat down uncomfortably on the edge of it, staring at him as if she didn't believe what she saw. Her eyes were too bright. They worried Paul. She said, "You didn't make him understand?"

Paul half smiled, not happily. "I don't think there's really anything in the world that boy doesn't understand. The point is, I didn't sell him anything. That's what I didn't do."

"Well, if you started out with that attitude, it isn't any wonder, is it?"

"I didn't have a choice of attitudes."

"Did you quarrel with him?"

Paul nodded regretfully. "I'm afraid I did."

She stood up with an explosive movement and crossed the short space between the couch and Paul's chair to stand over him, as if threatening. "Then nothing has changed. Not one thing has changed."

"Well, maybe things are a little worse."

"Why!" She threw her hands up in an actorish gesture and turned her back on him. She walked over to the room's one window and stared out for a time at the darkness. She said, more quietly, "Paul, why? I just can't understand why you had to quarrel with him."

"What you can't see, Elaine . . ." He stood up and moved a step toward her with the idea of taking her in his arms or something of the sort, but she gave him a stony look, sensing his intention, and he stopped before reaching her. He said, "There's nothing we can do but quarrel, Robert and I. He makes anything else impossible."

"*He! He* makes anything else impossible!" She pounded her fists softly three times on the windowsill. Paul felt each blow. "Paul, you're a grown man and he's only a little boy. *He* makes it impossible! Indeed! If you quarrel with him, it's because you want to quarrel with him, and for no other reason!"

"He asked me what you had done to persuade me to come crawling to him."

"Well, children are like that sometimes. They can be very cruel and blunt, but you have to remember that they're only children. You have to make allowances."

Paul shook his head again, sadly. "I've made all the allowances I can make. Too many, I'm very much afraid."

"I don't know what you mean by that."

"Elaine, I have very good reason to believe that something has happened up at the Academy. Something very bad, I'm afraid, and I think I have to tell you about it."

"If you plan to tell me something bad about Robert, you may as well save your breath. I won't believe a word you say. I won't listen to any more of your lies about Robert. I don't want to talk to you any more tonight."

"I think you'd better."

"Why are you constantly trying to turn me against Robert? Are you jealous of him or something?"

"Oh, come on, now, Elaine."

"Well, then, why? You never have a decent word to say about him. Never!"

"I try to get you to face facts, that's all." He was too tired to do very much more of this. "Just face a few facts here and there. But you never will, I guess."

"Paul."

"Yes?"

"If you can't get yourself straightened out about this, if you can't come to some kind of terms with Robert, you know what's going to happen, don't you?"

He knew perfectly well what she meant, but he had no intention of helping her to say it. "No."

"You'll have to go. I mean, I'll have to ask you to leave me. If you and Robert can't live together, then you're the one who will have to go. It's not what I ever want, but this is Robert's home, and Robert is my son."

Paul surprised himself by making a small laughing sound. It hadn't felt like laughter in his throat. "That's exactly what Robert told me not half an hour ago. But I don't think even he believed it would come so soon."

"No, I don't mean now!" She looked frightened, and it gave him some small satisfaction. "I don't mean now at all. I only mean, if you and Robert can't work things out."

"Then, it might just as well be now," Paul told her, "because we can't." Suddenly he could see Robert's smug face as plainly as if it were actually there before him, and he would have liked to slap it. "But first, by God, you're going to listen to me!" He took a long step toward her, and with only inches separating them, looked down at her steeply, dominating her at least with his extra inches of stature. But then, in the midst of the towering male superiority, it came to him that he was not only waging a losing battle but that he had no ammunition in his weapons. Until he heard from Al Dunlap, until he knew properly what he was talking about, he was firing blanks. "All right," he said, "forget it. Just forget it." He began picking at the top button of his shirt.

"Paul," Elaine said, "I want you to sleep in the library tonight."

"The library! I can sleep here in the study if you don't want me in your bed."

"No, Paul, the library. In here is too . . . it's too close."

"All right, God damn it!" He went out into the bedroom, still unbuttoning his shirt. Over his shoulder he said, "Any messages you'd like me to deliver to Stan, in case I see him down there?"

Chapter 10

PAUL AWAKENED AND lay on the couch for a time without moving, letting the unhappy circumstances of the awakening soak into his consciousness. His shorts, which he had worn instead of pajamas, were twisted in such a way as to make mutilation a danger if he moved. He had spent the night wrapped in a faded tan blanket that scratched. And it was Christmas morning! "Merry Christmas, Paul," he said with deep self-pity.

He pushed the blanket off and sat up on the edge of the couch, by some miracle escaping the mutilation threatened by the twisted shorts. They were still twisted, however, strangling him, and he had to stand up to get them straightened out and hanging normally. He remembered searching for bed clothing last night, determined not to go to Elaine for help, and finally finding the scratchy blanket in the second-floor linen closet. He had wondered at the time why there wasn't any linen in the linen closet. The reasoning behind it, of course, was feminine, and so not to be challenged.

Paul shivered. Everything about the library was cold. It was a hateful room, too long and too high for its width, ungraceful. The couch and chairs were upholstered in a chocolate-colored leather. The walnut desk occupied too much of the limited space and looked less austere than simply out of sorts. It had been polished too often and used too little. On the walls were untidy pen-and-ink sketches of a charging water buffalo and a lioness nursing her young, a charcoal drawing of a very angry old man, and a greatly enlarged photograph of Stan wearing a floppy hat and holding some kind of a fish by the tail. There was a single window in the narrow east wall and three along the north side. In the west wall was a door that opened onto the back lawn. Beside this was perhaps the most hateful thing in the whole room: the case that held Stan's collection of guns. Paul had always felt that Stan all but lived in this room, not as dead by half as was claimed for him. There was even an oddly unpleasant smell that Paul held Stan responsible for. A man who left a room like this didn't need a ghost to haunt the house he left it in.

He found his clothes laid not very neatly across the back of the leather armchair and began putting them on at once, wanting out of the room. Fastening his belt buckle, he walked to the back door and looked out. It had just begun to snow, dusting the brown lawn and the bare trees in the grove. It was going to be a white Christmas. Miserable but white. He hurt both his heels getting into his shoes because he had no shoehorn.

Elaine was in the living room fussing with the Christmas tree, putting in new lights or switching ornaments around or whatever it was she found to keep on doing. Robert and Stu were nowhere to be seen or heard. Elaine was looking somewhat forlorn. He couldn't be sure, but he thought her eyes were just a little puffy.

"Merry Christmas," he said quietly, realizing too late that, in the circumstances, it had a sarcastic ring.

"Oh!" She turned and smiled at him. A shade wanly? "Merry Christmas. I decided not to wake you up. There didn't seem to be any reason to. I mean . . ." This last quickly, as if to cover an unpleasant thought. "I mean, the boys aren't up yet, and breakfast won't be for a while."

"Elaine, about last night . . ."

"Please, Paul, can't we just put it off until tomorrow? I mean, after all, it *is* Christmas, and one more day won't make all that difference. I'd just rather not talk about it until tomorrow, if you don't mind."

"Well, as I said a minute ago, Merry Christmas."

"I'm sorry. I truly am."

Paul shrugged. "Do you think Laura has some coffee out there in the kitchen? I didn't sleep very well, and I don't think I want to try shaving without some coffee."

"I'll ask her."

"No, never mind. Go ahead with what you're doing. I'll find out for myself."

He went through the dining room to the kitchen and smelled coffee even before he pushed open the swinging door. Laura was standing in front of the wide white electric stove jabbing at something in a skillet. Her shoulderblades looked sharp enough to cut through the material of her uniform. Without turning, she said, "I'm afraid the sausages will get burnt if I don't take them up pretty quick now, Mrs. Hamilton."

Paul said, "It's Mr. Hamilton, Laura. Merry Christmas."

"Oh!" Laura whirled about now, holding a spatula as if to defend herself, should it become necessary. "Excuse me. I thought it was Mrs. Hamilton."

"That's all right. Can I have a cup of that coffee I smell?"

"Yes, sir. There's plenty for everybody, only it's not going to be very good, being made so long ago and everything. Oh, I forgot. Merry Christmas."

"Merry Christmas," Paul said again.

Laura went to the cupboard over the sink and took down one of the squat gray cups and a saucer to match it. "Where would you want me to serve the coffee, Mr. Hamilton?"

"Would it be all right if I just had it here?" Paul drew one of the chairs out from its place under the enameled table and sat down on it. "I'm not sure I can make it out of here without some coffee."

"Oh. Why, yes, sir." She didn't look very happy about it, though, Paul thought. "I'd better just take these sausages off the fire first. I guess they're ruined. I thought everybody'd be ready sooner."

While she took the skillet off the hot burner and poured his coffee, Paul said, "When I was a kid, I was up on Christmas morning practically before it got light."

"Yes, sir. Me too."

"I guess things have changed. Me or kids or Christmas or something."

"Yes, sir." Laura put the coffee on the table in front of him. "I'll just go see if there's anything I can do for Mrs. Hamilton."

"Laura." He had to say it quickly in order to catch her before she was out of the room. "You said you wanted to talk to me. Why don't you sit down and have a cup of coffee and do your talking now?"

Laura stood clumsily, her weight on one foot and her hand reaching out for the swinging door. She shook her head violently. "Not now, Mr. Hamilton," she whispered hoarsely. "Not with Mr. Robert in the house. I'll let you know when."

He wondered—and it was the first time this had ever happened to him—he wondered what he was doing in this house. He had now been rejected by everybody in it except Stu, who belonged here even more tenuously than he did. He knew perfectly well that this was maudlin thinking, but, damn it, a man had a right to feel sorry for himself when he was wronged, didn't he? He knew more about what was going on in this house than anybody else in it, and yet he was the one nobody would listen to.

He got up suddenly out of his chair, bumping the table and spilling his coffee over into the saucer, and went to the cupboard where he knew Laura kept the cooking sherry, rum, and brandy. He took the half-full brandy bottle back to the table with him and poured from it into the cup until there was no more room. "Well," he said aloud, "it's too God damn hot anyway."

Chapter 11

THE SNOW HAD turned fierce. It bore no kinship whatever to the large floating flakes, suitable for stuffing pillows, that people thought of as Christmas snow. It was fine and appeared too dry for snowballs or snowmen. Driven by an angry east wind, it came down at a forty-five-degree angle like so many millions of hurled weapons. It made drifts in corners and against trees, creating its own alien contours. It was bearing out to the letter, Paul thought, his prediction about the day: miserable but white.

Before a lively fire in the living room—it made the room a little too warm for Paul—the gift-opening ceremony had begun. Robert had already unwrapped a set of luggage, for which he had no use whatever but for which he had given Elaine a thank-you kiss. Stu was sitting at the farthest end of the couch, trying to keep his feet on the floor, feeling—or so it looked to Paul—like an intruder. Elaine was picking her way about among the packages, making selections, and she did not seem as gay as Christmases ordinarily made her. Paul was sorry about that. Honestly sorry. "Here's another one for you, Robert," she said. Her voice sounded too flat.

Robert left his place on the couch and went to Elaine, took the package from her, and kissed her cheek. From the shape of the box, Paul thought, it must be the gold pen-and-pencil set. Robert said to Elaine, "Did you wrap it too? I almost hate to open it, it looks so nice."

Paul was not sure whether the discomfort in his stomach was because of what was going on, because he had had three cups of strongly laced coffee, or because he had tried to put waffles and sausages in on top of them. Whatever the cause, the discomfort was there. And there was an odd feeling at the right corner of his mouth, as if it would start twitching if he gave it a chance. He was sitting in the chair to the left of the fireplace, sitting there stiffly, he was afraid, and not looking as jovial as the head of a family should look on Christmas day.

Robert had opened the pen-and-pencil set and was looking at it as though it were good enough to eat. "It's beautiful, Mother," he said. "Thank you very much."

"But, Bob," Stu said, "ain't you already got a pen and pencil?"

"That old thing?" Robert laughed. "You can have that."

"I already got one of my own," Stu said stiffly. He looked down at his hands, examining the nails with sudden interest. If he had been a few years younger, Paul thought, he might have burst into tears, perhaps without knowing exactly why. He looked so pathetic that Paul wished he had bought him the more expensive watch, the one with the days and months. "I gotta use ball-points, anyway," he said. "I push too hard for the other kind."

Elaine said, "I do hope we know somebody by the name of Stuart Parker." It was very heavy humor, Paul thought, not her style at all. "Because there's a package here for somebody by that name."

"Hey, that's me!" Stu said in an astonished voice.

Elaine lifted from the confusion of packages one that was a good deal too bulky to be either a watch or a box of ties. "Well, then, I guess you're the one who'll have to open it."

Stu bounced off the couch and came forward to accept his package. "How about that!" It seemed never to have occurred to him that they might have got a gift for him.

"It's from me," Robert said. "Go ahead, open it."

"Gee, thanks a lot!" Stu put the package down at his place

on the couch, and bending over it, worked the wrapping cord loose with clumsy fingers. He pushed the paper away to reveal a stack of comic books a good foot high. The cover of the top one displayed, without apparent shame, a very bad drawing of a figure in a long black cloak with a death's head peering—and without eyes, at that—out from beneath the cowl. "Hey, comic books!" Stu shouted. "About a million comic books! Gee, thanks a lot!"

"They all came out within the last week," Robert told him. "I didn't figure you'd have any of them yet. Not too many, anyway."

"Gee, thanks a lot!"

Elaine said, "Somebody must think a lot of you, Robert. Here's another one with your name on it."

Paul sat rigidly in his chair and tried not to let what he was feeling find its way into his face while Robert opened two more packages. One of them contained ski pants, a ski sweater, and cap. In the other was a pair of skis, the outrageous cost of which Paul remembered with pain. Robert was genuinely delighted; even Paul had to admit that.

"My father taught me to ski," he said proudly to Stu. He stood before the fireplace with the skis upright at his side. "He was very good." He said this to Stu, presumably, but looked at Paul.

Elaine smiled at Robert, the first really happy look she had given anybody all day. "I thought there must be skiing somewhere near the Academy."

Stu looked troubled. "There's a place somewhere, I'm pretty sure. I heard the guys talking about it."

"Putnam County," Robert said, "up near Beacon. It's about forty miles, but that's all right."

Stu's gift to Robert was a stereo album, on the cover of which was a photograph of some people with guitars, either young men or young women or both. They all had long hair and wore pants. "The Martians," Stu explained. "They're way out."

Robert nodded. " 'The Martian Motion' is on here. It's not bad at all."

Stu had brought a box of handkerchiefs for Elaine and a box of glass-encased cigars, his father's favorite brand, for Paul. Paul took a chance with his already disturbed stomach and lighted one of them. Elaine took one of the handkerchiefs out of her box and held it to her nose.

Speaking through the handkerchief, Elaine said, "That Stuart Parker is pretty popular around here. There are two more packages for him."

"But I got mine," Stu said.

"All the same . . ." Elaine said. She held the two packages out to him.

Stu came off the couch more slowly this time. His face was flushed. "I only got one for everybody."

Elaine touched his shoulder lightly and smiled at him, looking like the real Elaine. "Stuart, that isn't what matters. If people counted Christmas presents, what would become of Christmas? And even if you felt you just had to count, you gave presents to three people, and, from the way it looks, three people gave presents to you. What's wrong with that?"

"Oh, yeah. Well . . . yeah. Yes, ma'am."

And Elaine's smile turned sad, sad enough to break Paul's heart, and he didn't know why. She didn't look at him, but he knew it was somehow because of him. In all the world, the thing he wanted least of all was to make Elaine's smile sad.

Stu took the gay wrapping off the box of ties and did a very good job of looking pleased with them. Then, still seeming a little embarrassed, he plucked the ornate knot with which Elaine had tied up the watch box. Failing to untie it, he slipped the cord off the end of the package clumsily. He took the paper off as carefully as he could, and when he saw the rich grain of the leather box, opened his eyes very wide. He lifted the lid slowly. After a long pause, he said, "Jeepers!"

"What is it?" Robert asked him.

"It's a watch," Stu whispered.

"Well, you haven't got a watch."

"But . . . yeah, but . . ." Stu looked up first at Elaine and then at Paul. "It's the kind you don't even have to wind. I mean, it's got no stem."

"Do you like it?" Elaine asked him.

"Jeepers!"

Paul was pleased out of all proportion. "It's supposed to be waterproof and shockproof," he said. What he was trying to do, he realized, was let Stu know that it was he who had picked the watch out. A very childish thing.

"I never had anything like this, ever," Stu said. "I mean, I don't even know any grownups with watches like this. Do you, Bob?"

Robert laughed. "The kid's all broken up."

"Well, but . . . Jeepers!"

"There's one thing I have to tell you, Robert," Elaine said. "We just didn't have time to get your rifle." Robert's face hardened for the briefest moment. Elaine didn't seem to notice it. "I thought maybe you could pick it out yourself when we go into the city tomorrow."

"Are we going into the city tomorrow?" Robert asked her.

Elaine plucked a gaily striped envelope off the tree itself and handed it to Robert. "Here. Open it." She looked down at Stu, frowning a little. "I'm very embarrassed about it, to tell you the truth. It's two tickets for *I Lay Me Down.* That's a play, Stuart, and a very big hit. You have to get tickets just months in advance, and I ordered these before I knew you were coming home with Robert. So, you see, I only have two. Stuart?"

Stu was still examining his watch, the strap of which, he had found, fitted his fat wrist snugly, just right. He looked up at Elaine with preoccupied eyes and said, "Excuse me? Oh. Oh, that's all right, Mrs. Hamilton, I'd just as soon stay home and read my comic books anyway." He grinned. "And keep track of what time it is and everything."

"Maybe you could still get another ticket," Robert said. "You *would* like to come with us, wouldn't you, Stu?" Paul thought this last was oddly accented, as if, perhaps, it contained a secret message of some sort. "Wouldn't you, Stu?"

"Honest to gosh, Bob, I'd just as soon———"

"I'll call and see if there's anything available," Elaine said. "What we can do, if I'm able to get another ticket, you two can sit together and I'll take the odd seat."

Stu said, "Mrs. Hamilton, I wish you wouldn't . . ."

"We can decide about who sits where later on," Robert said.

Elaine moved toward the hall. "I'd better call right away. If I have any trouble, I'll get hold of Marge Kaplan. Her husband is a public-relations man of some kind, and he knows the producer or the director or the star or somebody in just about every show in town. I won't be long."

Stu said, "Mrs. Hamilton, I wish you wouldn't . . ." But Elaine was already out of the room.

Robert gave Stu a cold look. "What's all this, all of a sudden, you don't want to see a good play?"

"Bob, for Pete's sake, can't you see your mother wants to be alone with you for a little while? What kind of a creep do you take me for, tagging along everywhere?"

"Don't be stubborn, Stu. I want you to come with us."

Stu shook his head firmly. "I'm not going to."

"We'll see. We'll talk about it later."

They all sat in silence for what seemed a very long time, Robert eyeing Stu with disapproval, Paul pretending to stare into the fire but watching Robert, Stu looking at his new watch with love or something very like it. They could hear Elaine on the telephone in the hallway but could not understand what she was saying. The front-door chime sounded.

"Laura!" Elaine called.

They heard the front door open, and after a brief exchange between Laura and somebody with a boyish voice, close again. Elaine called from the hallway, "It's all right, Stuart; I got another seat. It's in the balcony, but that will be all right."

Nobody answered her.

There was more talking from the hallway, apparently between Elaine and Laura, and then Elaine came to stand just inside the living room, holding an open flower box in her arms. Paul could smell the roses all the way across the room.

"Robert," Elaine said, "I think you're the sweetest boy in the whole wide world!"

Robert smiled at her. "I'm glad they got here all right."

"Roses," Elaine said to Paul. "A dozen of them, with the longest stems you ever saw."

"I told them they had to be delivered before three o'clock this afternoon or the deal was off," Robert said. "I don't think they're very bright down there at the flower shop. How could I call the deal off? I'd already paid them."

Elaine bowed her head to smell the flowers. She said, "Stan used to have roses delivered to the house every Christmas afternoon."

Chapter 12

THE CHRISTMAS DINNER had seemed to be a great success, Elaine thought. Stuart, who was a very likable but a very funny little boy, had been so engrossed in his turkey breast, mashed potatoes, and cranberry sauce that he had taken time away from them for only an occasional glance at his wristwatch and not for anything else. She herself had chattered foolishly, knowing it at the time. "You remember that little Helen Strong, Robert? The skinny one? She's away at Bennington now, and according to Mrs. Marlow, just as pretty as a picture." And, "Didn't you know a boy by the name of Eberhart before you went away to Hastings? Charles, yes. Well, his father took a new job in Chicago, and they say . . ." She had almost forgotten the trouble with Paul, rattling away like that.

Stu had taken an armload of new comic books up to the guest room as soon as dinner was over, and Paul, pleading indigestion—

she knew all about the brandy with his morning coffee—had gone
upstairs to lie down. Elaine, almost as if it had been planned,
found herself alone with Robert.

They were in the living room. The snow was still falling, but
it was more gentle now. Not the raging thing it had been a little
earlier. Robert had just put a new log on the fire, and he stood
over it, making sure it caught. How very like his father Robert
was going to be! She could imagine Stan at thirteen, looking,
moving, talking, thinking almost exactly as Robert did. Not quite
exactly, of course; Robert seemed to go one step beyond Stan in
everything. Just a little more handsome, a little more brilliant,
a little more stern when circumstances warranted it, a little more
aloof with those who had not earned his warmth. It was a fine
thing, she thought, to be the mother of a boy like Robert.

Someday, she knew, Robert was going to marry, and she hoped
it would be the right girl. She didn't want to be one of those
mothers who thought nobody on earth was good enough for her
son, but she knew that the girl who married Robert would have to
have some special talents. She would have to resign herself—and
like it—to being ruled, as Elaine herself had been ruled by Stan.
She would have to learn to match herself to his moods—they had
been many in Stan's case—and to accept her role as a single and
separate factor in his life rather than as an integral part of the
whole. He would give her, as Stan had given Elaine, pride in his
bearing and his accomplishments; he would be a passionate lover
if she could match him desire for desire; but there were things—
Elaine would never have said as much aloud—that he would not
give her if he followed Stan's pattern: a share in his achievements,
a haven to rest in when rest was needed, the female satisfaction of
having molded the male at least a little. She would have to sub-
tract from the fine qualities those that suited a wife less perfectly
and settle for the net gain. Elaine had done so quite successfully
with Stan, and she felt it would be less, rather than more, difficult
with Robert.

Robert gave a final poke at the fire and turned to face her, still holding the poker. "You know what I'd bet? A million dollars? You're going to ask me to wear my uniform tomorrow."

"Oh, but, Robert, you look so handsome in it."

"It's like a mechanic wearing coveralls."

Elaine sighed. "Of course, if you feel you just can't stand to go into the city wearing the uniform, then I won't insist. It's just one of those mother things. Pride and all that. Still . . ."

Robert put the poker back in its rack and came to stand in front of her. She was sitting on the couch, and to have him standing there looking down at her that way almost made her feel that Stan had returned, that time had somehow got turned back. Of all the many things Stan had left her, she thought, this was the most precious, this boy, this replica of himself. Stan, perhaps, had not been quite the perfect husband. She could admit that to herself. He had had more than a little of the despot in him. He had had more enemies than friends because of it, she felt sure. He had dominated her absolutely; she was aware of that. Still, those people were wrong who believed—Paul, most particularly—that Robert dominated her in his turn. She truly believed that they were wrong. It was Stan's personality, surviving through Robert, that dominated her, if anything did. That and her great love for Robert.

Robert said, "I'll bet my father couldn't refuse you a thing, could he?" He stooped in that graceful way of his and kissed her forehead. "All right." He sat down beside her on the couch. "If it's really that important to you, I'll wear the silly uniform."

"It's the most amazing thing," Elaine said. It *was* amazing. "I've heard those exact words from your father, I don't know how many times. 'If it's that important to you . . .' It's what he always used to say."

Robert leaned back and put his arm along the back of the couch behind Elaine. Neither of them spoke for a time. Robert had that faraway look of his father's, and Elaine knew that he was thinking about something he considered important. At last he said, "Don't misunderstand me, Mother, but don't you sometimes feel . . ."

He turned to look at her, into her eyes. "Doesn't it seem dull sometimes, being married to . . . *him*?"

"No," Elaine said, "no, I can't say that. It's a *different* sort of life, yes, but that doesn't mean it has to be a bad sort."

"I just don't see how . . . well, never mind."

"We do love each other, Robert, Paul and I. It's possible to love one man without being unfaithful to the memory of another."

Robert shook his head, almost imperceptibly.

"You're so very young, Robert. It's easy to forget that, because you're also very adult in many ways, but you *are* young."

"I'll be glad when people stop saying that."

"I'm sorry."

"Oh, well. Is there any Coke in the refrigerator?"

"I expect so."

Robert stood up. "Can I bring you one? Or something else?"

"No, thank you."

Robert went to the opening and said, over his shoulder as he disappeared into the hallway, "If I'm not back in a couple of minutes, better come looking for me. Laura may try to run me through with a carving knife or something."

Elaine sat waiting for Robert and wondering if there were anything she had left undone in her effort to bring him and Paul together. She could think of nothing. She knew, of course, that it was not entirely Paul's fault that they felt this way about each other. Not quite entirely. She knew that Robert could be difficult at times. Whatever Paul thought, she believed that she was capable of being quite unbiased in her appraisal of Robert. She knew that he was moody and that, at least in Paul's case, he had a tendency to hold a grudge. Still, and especially since the night before last, it did seem to her that it was Paul who was trying to force a crisis.

Robert came back into the room with a tall glass full of ice and Coca-Cola. She liked that. So many of the boys these days liked to drink Coca-Cola right from the bottle, but Robert wanted his Coke in a glass with ice. He had such good taste in so many little things. He held the glass out to her and said, "Just a sip?"

"No, thanks."

He sat down beside her again and drank deeply from the glass. "I was thirsty. You know something? Laura didn't even threaten me."

"Robert," Elaine said, making her voice as untroubled as she could, "have you and Paul had any words? You know, any unpleasantness or anything like that?"

Robert stared at her over the rim of his glass and swallowed before speaking. "There hasn't been any pleasantness, I can tell you that. And the little talk last night didn't help, Mother."

"No, before that," Elaine said. "The night you got here."

"I didn't even talk to him that night." Robert frowned. "Why? Has something happened?"

"No, no. At least, not really."

Robert smiled at her. "That's strictly a mother answer."

"Well, actually, I guess it was just more something I felt than anything else." She certainly had no intention of telling Robert that Paul had wanted to cart him off to a psychiatrist. "It was when you and Stuart went up to your room to play your records. You remember? After dinner?"

"Yes."

"And when you played the music so loud—it *was* too loud, you know, Robert. Just ear-splitting."

"I'm sorry. I didn't realize."

"Well, anyway, Paul went upstairs to ask you to turn it down."

"Oh? He did?"

"Anyway, the music stopped. I mean, the record seemed to end. And then in a little while Paul came back downstairs, and he seemed just terribly upset."

Robert spread his arms in a gesture meant to imply innocence. "I didn't even see him."

"Yes, that's what he told me later. But he was terribly upset, all the same."

"Now, wait a minute." Robert put his glass down on the coffee table and twisted about on the couch so that he faced her. "He was upstairs when the record ended? The one that was too loud?"

"That's right."

"What did he say?"

"I don't know what you mean."

"When he came back downstairs. What did he say when he came back downstairs?"

"Oh. Well, I don't really remember. I guess nothing really specific. He was just . . . terribly upset."

Robert said, "Of all the lousy luck!"

"What?"

"Oh. I mean, to have something upset him just at a time like this. When we were hoping, you know, that we might be able to get things straightened out." He reached, almost shyly, for her hand and covered it with his own. "But we weren't going to get things straightened out anyway, Mother."

"Robert, I can't understand why both of you have this attitude. This defeatist attitude."

Robert sighed. "I'm sorry, Mother, but I think we have to have a serious talk, you and I."

"All right. I mean, I think that's a very good idea."

"I know, of course, that you and Paul are married and everything, and I don't want to interfere." His voice was soft and extraordinarily persuasive. Elaine was appalled to realize that she was reminded of her most intimate moments—her very most intimate—with Stan. "Maybe I'm just being selfish," Robert went on, "but I really think you ought to know this."

"Know what, dear?"

"I hate to make you any unhappier than you are."

"If there's something you think I ought to know . . ."

"There is." Robert patted her hand and took his own away. "I think Paul is trying to get rid of me."

"Get . . . rid of you?"

"Yes. Oh, I don't know how far he'd go. I don't think he has the nerve to—you know—kill me. All the same, I'm not ruling it out completely."

"Robert!"

"I'm sorry, Mother. The thing is, I think he sees me as a threat. You said he loves you, and I'm sure he does. He loves you so much that he isn't going to let anything stand between you and him. And no matter how hard I try to make him see he's wrong, he thinks of me as something that *does* stand between you and him. So he thinks he has to get rid of me."

"Robert, do you know what you're saying!"

"Yes, I do, Mother." Robert lowered his head and rubbed his eyes with the tips of his fingers. It was, ironically, a characteristic gesture of Paul's. "I've known about this for a long time; it's no surprise to me. But how could I come to you with it? You kept on telling me how much you loved Paul. How could I come to you and say, 'Your husband that you love so much hates my guts and means to get rid of me, one way or another'? How could I come to you and say a thing like that?"

"Oh, no, Robert!"

With his right hand, Robert took her chin and turned her head so that she had to face him. "I don't think he aims to kill me, Mother; I honestly don't. If only because he doesn't have the nerve. I think he plans to—what's the word?—discredit me. I think he plans to come to you with some ridiculous story about me —maybe with faked evidence; I don't know—and turn you completely against me, once and for all. He may even think he can get me committed or something, for all I know. I'm not like most kids my age. Maybe it wouldn't be too hard to make out a case like that against me."

And Paul had wanted to send Robert to a psychiatrist, Elaine remembered. To one he had already selected? To an accomplice? Paul, do such a thing? "It's so hard to believe!" she moaned.

Robert touched her hand with a fingertip. "I know."

The thing was, although Elaine had never considered her problem a simple one, she had always thought of it as more or less a marriage-counselor kind of problem, one with a soap-opera theme, and so one that ought to have a soap-opera ending. Now, for the very first time, she was frightened.

"Please don't look like that, Mother," Robert said. "I told you, I don't think he aims to kill me."

"We have to get out of here!"

"What!"

"Well, if he's threatened you, and . . ."

"No!" He stood up. "That's no good." He went to the front window and looked out, frowning. The snow was sticking to the window now, she noticed irrelevantly. Robert faced her again and said, "No, that's no good." He came back to stand in front of her, frowning down at her. "Would my father run away? Besides, that would only let him know we're on to him. It would only bring things to a head before we're ready."

"Oh," Elaine said. "No, I don't want that."

"Then, let's just go on as if nothing had happened." Robert made a blank of his face and then smiled, looking, she thought, more like her Robert. "At least there are no secrets between us now. And it's the best thing—just to go on as if nothing had happened."

"Are you sure?"

"I try to be like my father. He was always sure."

"Don't you think I ought to talk to Paul?"

"About what?"

"Well . . . all this."

Robert shook his head bleakly. "It's not that kind of a game, Mother. We don't tell him anything; he doesn't tell us anything. That's the kind of game it is."

"All right, then, I won't tell him any of this that we've been talking about, but I still want to see him."

"What about?" Robert said sharply.

"Robert! After all!"

"I'm sorry, Mother. Are you sure you can talk to him without letting anything slip? Any of this that we've been talking about?"

"For goodness' sake," Elaine said, but she smiled at him. "Who's the parent here, and who's the child?"

"I just hope you'll be careful, that's all." He rubbed his hand over his chin, the way his father had always done, as if there were a stubble there. "All right." It sounded very much like a permission granted.

They went up the stairs together, and Robert stood at the head of the stairway watching her as she opened the master-bedroom door and peeped inside. She backed away and closed the door again quietly. "He's asleep," she said to Robert. "I won't wake him up just now."

Robert shook his head over this, smiling. "All right, let him sleep, then. I want to talk to Stu about something. I'll be down in a few minutes."

Stu was in the guest room, curled up tightly on the bed, reading a comic book nearsightedly. It was a formal room, and Stu looked out of place in it. Robert went in without knocking. Stu looked up, only a little startled, and said, "Oh, hi."

Robert sat on the edge of the bed and said, "About the play tomorrow, Stu. I think you'd better come with us."

"What for? Pete's sake, what are you making such a federal case out of it for?"

"I don't want to leave you alone here with him." Robert pointed back toward the master bedroom. "I don't trust you."

"That's a fine thing to say to a guy."

"If you're planning something, I'll find out about it. You know that, don't you, Stu?"

"What the heck's the matter with you, anyway? Why do I have to be planning something? I'm planning to read a mess of comic books, that's what I'm planning. Pete's sake!"

"It would be better all around if you came with us."

"Well, I'm not gonna, and that's all there is to it."

"All right, but he's going to be here all day. If you blab to him, Stu, I swear I'll kill you. I mean that. Not just a stupid game. I'll kill you."

"Aw, come off it, Bob. You gotta stop talking like that."

"All right. Just watch yourself, that's all."

"So I'll watch myself."

Leaving Stu's door open, Robert went to his own room. He went straight to his bed, lifted the mattress, and took the thick leatherbound notebook from under it. He carried this to his desk, sat down, and opened it to a clean page. He took his new gold pen out of its box and began writing in the book.

Chapter 13

ELAINE SAID, "I'M sorry, but I have to wake you up. This can't wait any longer."

Paul lay on his back and looked up at her, trying to focus. He had a strong feeling that her voice had cut a nightmare off in mid-career, although he was unable to remember any of its details. The same nightmare, quite possibly, to which she had awakened him. He struggled with the sluggish remnants of sleep and was able to sit up. He said, "What can't wait any longer?"

Elaine had straightened and moved back a step to give him room to sit on the edge of the bed. "I'm sorry," she said again. "You'll have to go, Paul. There's no other way that I can see now. You'll just have to go."

"Go where?" The conversation seemed to have begun in the middle. "I don't know what you're talking about."

"It doesn't matter where. I mean, I suppose it does, but that's not the point. You have to go away from here."

"What!"

"Now. Right away."

"What the hell are you talking about?"

"You can take the Cadillac. I'll be all right with the station wagon. You can just pack what you need for now. I'll help you. I imagine you can get a room at the Gladstone. You always liked the Gladstone, didn't you? Or have they torn that down? Yes, I think they have. Anyway——"

"Shut up!"

"Paul!"

"Oh, for God's sake." Paul pushed himself up off the bed, and Elaine took another backward step. His shorts were twisted again. He was damned if he was going to loosen his trousers and straighten them out with Elaine standing there. "What's happened?"

"Happened?"

"What's he told you now?"

"Told me? Who?"

"Who the hell do you think? Robert, of course." He was so angry it almost felt good. "What's he said about me now?"

"I didn't say he'd said anything."

"Oh, for the love of God, Elaine, do you think I'm that stupid? Who besides Robert could make you talk to me like this? Who else would want to?"

"Now, wait a minute," Elaine said. "What are you getting so hot under the collar about? What's anybody done to you?"

"What's anybody done to me! You've just finished telling me to pack up and get the hell out, and you want to know what anybody's done to me! For Christ's sake, Elaine, what's the matter with you?"

"Don't talk to me that way!"

"All right." Paul was honestly sorry about cursing at her. He took a step toward her, thinking that if he could touch her, make her understand that he was the same Paul he had always been, things would be better, would be all right. She backed away from him. "A man's taking a nap after his Christmas dinner, and his wife comes in and yells 'Get out' at him, and you don't think he deserves some kind of explanation?"

Elaine frowned. "I want to be fair about this."

"That'll make a nice change."

"Now, stop that!" She turned half away from him. "Oh, Paul, why do you have to hate the boy so much?"

There was no profit in denying the charge, he decided. Not at this point. "Well, primarily, I suppose, because he hates me. And because he doesn't give a damn how unhappy you are or what becomes of you at all. Oh, I know, you don't see that. He's nothing but Mama's little angel whenever you're around."

"Paul!"

"But it's true, all the same. And I don't like him because in that calculating way of his, he's managed to do this to us, you and me. Have you ever asked him why he hates me?"

"He doesn't hate you. He . . ."

"Tell me what he said about me to make you want me to leave so suddenly."

Elaine faced him, stood as tall as she could, and looked him straight in the eye. "I promised Robert I wouldn't."

"All right, I'll make *you* a promise. You're going to have one hell of a time getting me out of here without telling me."

"Paul, I wish you'd stop swearing."

"Dear God! The world's coming to an end, and you're upset because I said a bad word."

Still looking him in the eye, Elaine said, "All right. Robert knows you plan to get rid of him."

"Get rid of him!"

"He doesn't believe you'd go so far as to kill him, but maybe that's just because he's too charitable. If I believe any of it . . . I mean, once you start believing in horrors, where do you stop?"

"God Almighty!"

"I'm frightened, Paul. So is he."

"Of me? Robert is frightened of me?"

"Yes, he is, although he puts up a very brave front. What you refuse to recognize, Paul, is that he's still a boy. A child. It would be bad enough if you meant to . . . to get rid of a grown man, but to . . . He's just a boy yet, Paul."

She looked so embattled and so courageous in the face of it that Paul's anger couldn't stand against it, no matter what she said. He moved toward her again, reached out for her, aware of the clumsiness with which he moved.

She said, "No, Paul. That kind of thing won't do any good."

He let his arms drop to his sides. "Do you honestly believe that I'd . . . that I *could* do anything like that?"

"Robert says you could."

Suddenly his anger was back, redoubled. "And if Robert says so, then it has to be gospel, is that it? No matter how often he proves himself to be a liar and a cheat and a stinking egotistical little bastard who doesn't give a damn in this world about you or anybody else, still you'd rather believe me capable of murder than admit to yourself that he just might have told you a lie."

"That's quite enough of that, Paul."

"All right."

"You'll go?"

"I'll go." He turned his back on her, unzipped his trousers, and straightened out his shorts, speaking at the same time. "But I won't go tonight. I'm expecting a very important phone call, and I have to be here to take it. Tomorrow." He had no idea how to go about reaching Al Dunlap. "It's very important."

"A phone call from whom?"

"Under the circumstances, I think I'm justified in telling you it's none of your God-damn business. As soon as the call comes in tomorrow, I'll get out and maybe even be glad to go, but in the meantime, you'll just have to put up with me."

Elaine sighed. "I'm sorry, Paul."

"To hell with sorry. Where can I find some sheets? I slept last night under a lousy woolen blanket and nothing else, and I don't intend to sleep that way again tonight. Just tell me where you keep the God-damn sheets."

Elaine said, "I want you to sleep here tonight, Paul."

"In the name of God, why?"

She hesitated a moment and then said, "So I can watch you."

Chapter 14

"GOOD MORNING." PAUL stepped into the dining room, and although he could not quite bring himself to try a smile, he did try not to look unpleasant. Not to look, in fact, murderous. "I'm sorry I'm late."

Elaine said, "Oh!" She was badly flustered, and it gave Paul an unsatisfactory kind of satisfaction. "I think Laura's fixing a tray to take upstairs to you. I mean, I thought . . ."

"Better tell her not to bother. I'm not up there." Paul sat down stolidly at his usual place. "I can use some of that coffee."

"Yes," Elaine said, "I'd better tell her."

"I'll go," Stu said and hopped out of his chair. He took one of Laura's little biscuits off his plate and bit into it as he disappeared into the hallway.

"Have you almost finished, Robert?" Elaine said; and then to Paul, "I didn't think you'd be coming down this morning."

"I decided I would." A strange mood had got hold of Paul. A perverse mood. He didn't want to be the only miserable person in the house. He had lost, but he was determined not to be the only loser. One thing he knew: if he left, and he could see no way to avoid it, he did not intend to make a disorganized scramble of his going. Defeat was one thing; flight was quite another. It was a

very childish way of thinking, he supposed, but he had to look
somewhere for comfort.

Stu came back in, walking very slowly and carrying with the
greatest caution a plate of bacon and eggs. "I told her I'd bring
them in," he said, looking down half crosseyed at the plate. "I
caught her just in time." He put the plate down at Paul's place and
sighed his relief. "There's no more hot biscuits, though, unless
she mixes up a whole new batch."

"That won't be necessary."

As Stu sat down again, Robert said, "I have a very good suggestion, I think."

Elaine smiled at him with a brightness that Paul recognized—
and because of his odd mood this morning, he was glad—as thoroughly false and not altogether attractive. "What is it, dear?"

"You remember that place in Vermont, that ski lodge where my
father used to take us?"

Elaine said, "If you mean Perrin's Lodge, yes."

"I think so, yes." There was an extraordinary softness in
Robert's expression, a believable softness. "They had a fireplace
three times as big as ours. Downstairs, you know, in the lobby or
whatever they called it. There was one slope for beginners and
then the steep one for people who knew what they were doing.
My father always took me on the steep slope. I never once went
down the one they meant for beginners."

Elaine nodded, smiling now as if she meant it. "That's Perrin's
Lodge, all right. You were just a little boy then, Robert. I'm
surprised you remember it at all."

"I remember everything," Robert told her. "Anyway, I heard on
the radio that skiing conditions are excellent in Vermont. I'd like
to spend a day up there. I want to try out my new skis."

"Well," Elaine said, "today, of course . . ."

"Oh, not today." Robert reached across the table and touched
his mother's arm. "Tomorrow. We have a theater date today." He
turned to Paul. "You'll come with us, won't you?"

"No."

"No?" Robert's smile grew slowly, dripping superiority. "Don't you ski? Not at all?"

"I ski," Paul said. "I ski, all right." He looked quickly at Elaine and quickly away again. His mood was breaking up, leaving him defenseless. "I think tomorrow I have to go into the city. There are still some things to iron out with Mr. Mosely. At my publishers, you know."

"Publishers!" Stu said. "Did you write a book or something?"

"It'll never make the comics, I'm afraid." Paul smiled an honest smile at Stu. "It's a textbook."

"Oh."

"I may be tied up for some time, as a matter of fact. There's a good chance I won't be seeing you boys again before you have to get back to the Academy."

"It's very important, a book coming out," Elaine said.

"I was hoping you'd come with us," Robert said.

What, Paul wondered, has he got in his sneaky little mind now? He said, "Well, actually, this matter is pretty urgent." He could not resist turning to Elaine and adding, "Isn't it?"

"The thing is," Robert said, "I don't imagine Mother and Stu will want to try the steep slope. I thought maybe we could try it together, you and I. It gives people a very close feeling, you know, skiing together."

"Robert?" Elaine looked terribly distressed.

"Mother, may I see you alone for a minute?"

Elaine glanced nervously first at Paul and then at Stu. "That's not very polite, is it, Robert?"

"Go ahead," Paul said to them. "You don't have to be polite to Stu and me."

Elaine followed Robert out into the hallway, leaving Stu and Paul alone, Stu to scoop up the last yellow bit of his last egg, Paul to puzzle over this newest thing of Robert's. What it was not, of course, was a gesture of friendship; that was very certain to Paul. A general who has just won a war rarely capitulates instead of accepting his opponent's surrender. When he does, it behooves the opponent to examine very closely the terms of the capitulation.

Either idiocy or some Machiavellian strategy must be back of it, and Paul was not prepared to consider Robert an idiot.

Stu wiped his mouth and his hands with a messy napkin, selecting the clean spots with meticulous care. "I've finished," he told Paul. "If you'll excuse me, I guess I'll just go on up to my room." He grinned. "I left Captain Galaxy in an awful mess."

"Stu," Paul said, "Did you ever read *Tom Sawyer* or *Huckleberry Finn?*"

"We get *Huckleberry Finn* next term in English 1-A. Bob says it's kind of icky."

Paul nodded. "That figures."

Elaine and Robert came back into the dining room, and Paul noticed that Elaine looked different. Thoughtful but not unhappy.

"You finished, Stu?" Robert asked.

"Yeah, I was just gonna go on upstairs."

"Okay, come on."

The two of them left, Robert striding ahead, Stu half trotting after him.

"I think you'd better come with us, Paul," Elaine said.

"Skiing?"

"Robert seems to have his heart set on it."

"Well, then, that settles it, doesn't it?"

"Please don't, Paul. Robert wants to make friends with you. No, I mean, he really does. I don't know how far you've gone with this . . . this way you feel about him, but he thinks that, out there where everything is so clean and, you know, crisp and white, it just might work out."

Paul smiled at her sadly. "And you believe that, don't you? You really do."

"I do, yes."

"Aren't you afraid I'll bury him in the snow or something? Or start an avalanche?"

"I know I've hurt you, Paul," she said. "I'm sorry. I'm just groping and . . . won't you please come with us tomorrow, Paul?"

Recognizing one more small defeat, Paul said, "All right. I guarantee you, it's not what Robert says it is, but if you really want me to, I'll come."

"You have to understand," Elaine said, "that I don't want to lose you, either."

Chapter 15

THE SNOW THAT had fallen with such violence yesterday lay inert now, for there was no wind to give it life. It did not have the look of a substance that would later turn soupy and eventually melt away. It looked permanent. The day was gray and bitterly cold.

Paul backed the station wagon down the driveway to Shore Road for Elaine, and it was treacherous work in spite of the snow tires. Elaine thanked him formally, allowed Robert to help her into the car, and drove away without a backward look. Paul had meant to wish them a pleasant day in the city, but they were gone before he had the chance. He watched them out of sight and then walked back up the driveway in the tire tracks and went into the house by the library door, which was the nearest to the driveway. He kicked off his galoshes and put them down beside the door, where they would, of course, melt a puddle on the library carpet. He didn't care. He had struggled out of his fleece-lined overcoat before he realized that Laura was standing in the doorway that opened off the living room.

"What is it, Laura?"

She slipped into the library with a quick sidling movement and closed the door softly. "Are they gone?"

"Mrs. Hamilton and Robert? Yes."

"That Mr. Stuart's up there in the guest room, but I guess that's all right. So can I speak to you?"

"Oh. Yes, of course." The corner of Paul's mouth began to twitch. It had felt since last night on the verge of it, but now it actually twitched, and he couldn't stop it. He had never felt anything quite like it before. He pressed his fingertips against it. "Go ahead."

"Is something wrong, Mr. Hamilton? I mean, you don't look like you felt so good."

"I'm fine." Paul took his hand away from his mouth. A nervous tic, he knew, felt a thousand times more noticeable than it actually was. "I haven't been having one of my best days, but I'm perfectly all right."

"Well, I just have to talk to you, Mr. Hamilton. I don't mean to bother you, but I'll never get another chance like this."

"It's all right, Laura." He realized that she was a good deal more nervous than he, whether she had a tic or not. He began to feel sorry for her, and that, he decided, was a lot better than feeling sorry for himself. "Why don't you sit down? Take that chair." He nodded toward the leather armchair that faced the desk. He went around the desk and sat in the stiff chair behind it. He wondered if Stan would haunt him for the impertinence. "You don't have to feel unnatural or embarrassed talking to me, you know," he said to Laura. "I mean, I wish you wouldn't."

She sat on the front edge of the chair as though she expected to have to jump and run at any moment. There was something vaguely birdlike about her, Paul thought. As if she had just fallen out of her nest. "I don't know how to tell you," she said.

"Well, why not just out with it? It's about Robert, I suppose?"

She looked surprised. "Yes, sir. I couldn't speak to Mrs. Hamilton about it, or I didn't think I ought to. There's just nobody but you I can talk to."

"All right, Laura. Go ahead and do it."

"Well . . . okay, I guess. The thing is, Mr. Robert stole some money from me."

"He what!"

Laura nodded solemnly. "It was my payday. Just a couple of weeks before Mr. Robert went off to that school last fall. Mrs. Hamilton had paid me in cash that week, like she does sometimes when I can't get to the bank in time to cash a check. I had the money in my purse on the dresser in my room. It was night, see. I mean like maybe nine o'clock or half past. So about that time I had to go to the . . ." She looked down at her primly folded hands, and Paul thought a little tinge of improbable color touched her face. "I stepped out of my room for a minute. When I came back, I saw Mr. Robert just coming out of my door. I yelled at him and asked him what he was doing in my room, and he said he wasn't in there. I saw him coming out, and he said he wasn't in there, just as barefaced as you please." She stopped and looked at Paul, her head cocked a little to one side, waiting for a comment.

"And then what? You said he stole some money."

"Yes." She had a birdlike way even of nodding her head, a sharp pecking motion. "I went in my room and right first off I looked in my purse, because, Mr. Hamilton, a week's pay is very important to a working girl like me."

"A week's pay is important to anybody."

"Well, it wasn't there," Laura said flatly. "He took it."

"Now, let's just examine that for a minute," Paul said, trying to sound fair. "It looked as if he took it, yes, but you couldn't be absolutely certain, could you?"

She sat up even straighter, which he wouldn't have thought possible, and looked at him boldly. "Why couldn't I? I was in the john five minutes, maybe less, and when I came out, there was Mr. Robert sneaking out of my room. And my money was gone out of my pocketbook. Who do you think took it, if he didn't?"

"All right," Paul said, "all right, Laura; there's nothing to get excited about."

"Well, the way I look at it . . . okay, I'm sorry, Mr. Hamilton. Anyway, he finally admitted he took the money."

"He admitted it!"

She nodded. "I asked him about it the next day and he said, sure, he took it, so what. He said if I mentioned it to you or to Mrs. Hamilton, he'd kill me."

"Good God!"

"That's what he said, Mr. Hamilton, and he meant it. He still means it, too. I told him I'd forget all about it and quit my job and leave here, but he said no. He said he wanted me here where he could keep an eye on me. He said if I left he'd be sure to find me wherever I went to and he'd kill me." Her voice began to thin out, and a tremor was creeping into it. "And the thing is, I think he would. You know him, Mr. Hamilton. Don't you think he would?"

Paul sat quite still for a time, while Laura blew her nose. As she told it, of course, it sounded like nothing so much as a boy frightening a not very bright maid for the sheer pleasure of frightening her. But when you added it to Johnny Spence, what did it give you? When you added further Robert's malicious lies of last night to his mother, what did that give you? Well, actually, nothing much but a very strong suspicion, which was precisely what you had had from the start.

"Well, don't you think he would?" Laura asked again.

Paul sighed. "Boys sometimes play stupid, sadistic games, Laura. Nasty little games, meant to hurt grownups. Why they do it is a great mystery, I'll admit, but they're still only games."

"No, sir, Mr. Hamilton! Let me tell you——"

"Now, wait a minute, Laura. All I'm doing is just trying to think the whole thing through. Isn't that what you wanted me to do? Isn't that why you came to me?"

Laura looked dissatisfied but stopped protesting.

"Who knows what's going on in Robert's mind? Maybe he's just softening you up so he can steal from you again—if he really did steal from you the first time. No, wait until I've finished. It may be he even imagines—a kind of daydream, you know—that he actually would kill you if you disobeyed him. Or maybe . . ." Trying to make it look casual, Paul moved his right hand up to his mouth again; the tic was worse. "Or maybe he really does mean to go through with it. I don't know."

"Well, then, you have to do something, don't you? Like call the police or something?"

Paul considered this for a time and then said, "And what if it turns out to be just a little game he plays, as I suggested?"

"Don't you believe it for a minute. Besides, he stole my money, didn't he?"

"You don't have any proof of that." He had almost said, *"We* don't have any proof," implying a choice of sides. "Anyway," he went on, "I don't believe in having a boy sent away someplace just because a full purse tempted him once. If nobody ever got a second chance, we'd all be in trouble, wouldn't we?"

"It was my purse the money came out of, Mr. Hamilton. Why do I have to pay for his second chances?"

"I'll give you the amount you think he took from you," Paul said stiffly, "if that's all that's troubling you."

Laura looked down at her unlovely lap and moved her hand in a slow negative. "I don't care about the money anymore. I'm scared. You can sit there and make speeches about games and like daydreams and not sending kids away and all that, but I'm scared I'm going to get killed. If somebody threatens to kill you, isn't that reason enough to have them locked up?"

"I don't think you could do it, anyway, Laura. Not without at least something like proof."

"Okay."

There was a moment of overladen silence before Paul said, "What do you mean by 'okay'? Do you mean you have some kind of proof?"

Laura nodded. "He writes everything down in this diary of his, I found out. All kinds of things, he writes down. It's all in there about me. Killing me and everything. And it don't read like any little game, Mr. Hamilton. That's why I finally came to you; what have I got to lose?"

"How do you know what's in Robert's diary, Laura?"

"Because I read it, that's how. I found out that he keeps it under the mattress in his room, and I sneaked in there when you were all having dinner and read it."

Paul said softly, "That isn't a very nice thing to do, is it, Laura?"

"Mr. Hamilton, he's threatened to kill me, and I got a right to protect myself any way I can. If he can take all my money out of my room, why can't I read something out of a book he keeps under his mattress?"

Paul nodded reluctantly. "It's a good point."

"So?" Laura looked at him for a time, as though she had said everything she felt needed to be said. When he only sat on silently, she frowned and spoke impatiently. "Okay. Will you come and look at the diary yourself, Mr. Hamilton?"

He smiled gently and shook his head. "I don't think so, no."

Laura sat up very straight again, and there was something rather impressively like dignity in her bearing. "Mr. Hamilton, I don't like to go sneaking into people's bedrooms and peeping under mattresses and reading diaries any more than you do. I was brought up better than that. But when you've been . . ." She leaned a little forward, and a wheedling expression washed the dignity out of her face. "Look, what if I told you there's a lot of other stuff in there? Stuff about you, for one thing. All kinds of just awful stuff. I mean, I think you *got* to look in that book, Mr. Hamilton. Even forget about me; I think you *got* to."

Paul pressed his finger against the right corner of his mouth and thought about this. He asked himself whether, if he, Paul, kept a diary of all his most private thoughts and plans and actual deeds, Robert would read it and use its contents to his advantage. The answer was so clear it almost made him laugh. He said to Laura, "I don't know; maybe you have a point there, too."

"We could go up there and look at it right now," Laura said, pressing what she recognized as an advantage. "I mean, I don't think we'll ever get another chance like this."

Paul nodded and pushed himself up out of the chair. "It makes me a little sick, but I'm afraid we're going to have to do it."

Laura stood up, thrusting her head a little forward like a chicken again. "We'll have to watch out Mr. Stuart don't catch us, that's all." Lifting her knees high and walking on the tips of her toes like somebody in a Charlie Chaplin comedy, she moved out of the library, through the living room, and into the hallway, looking back from time to time to make sure he was behind her. He followed her as quietly as he could without making a silent two-reeler of it.

There was a moment just outside the door of Robert's room when the logic that had brought him this far failed him, leaving only a feeling of distasteful involvement. He hesitated for a moment, trying to decide whether or not to turn back. But Laura had already tiptoed into the room, and it was actually his reluctance to abandon her there that made him continue. He slipped into the bedroom, feeling as melodramatic as Laura had looked.

He stopped just inside the door and struggled with a sudden desire to laugh, which was probably half hysterical. Beside the bed, Laura was bent almost double, one hand holding up the mattress and the other searching frantically beneath it. It was a *New Yorker* cartoon, lacking only a caption.

Laura drew her arm out from under the mattress and carefully lowered the mattress to its support. In her hand was a looseleaf notebook of pliable black leather. She straightened slowly as though afraid her back would make a noise, and turning, nodded to Paul as if to say, "I told you so." She opened the book and flipped blank pages from the back toward the front until she came to the last entry. As she read this, her eyes widened, and having finished it, she looked up at Paul, her expression an improbable mixture of fear and smugness. She flipped one more page to the final entry but one. "This is the one about me," she whispered. She held the open book out to Paul.

He accepted it with distaste but with no further soul-searching. He was here, he had watched Laura ferret the book out of its hiding place, and he was thoroughly committed. What he was doing was no worse, in any case, than what Robert had done to him last night. He looked down at the book and read:

December 25:

Seem to have saddled myself with Stu over the holidays
for nothing. Can't risk two while I'm here and feel I must
give Laura priority. She's been through my room again.
Stupid bitch doesn't even know how to cover her tracks. And
she's been at my mother's husband about something, that's
clear enough. So Laura goes. Save Stu for later. He'll be
around all the rest of the lousy year at the Academy. Two
within the year there? Challenge. Method for Laura?

Down the stairs—steep but not certain at all.

Out the window—better but ditto.

Rifle—sure but ballistics and all that crap.

Strangle—untried but exciting. Think over.

What would my father have done? Anyway, better than
a week to go. Plenty of time to think over.

Laura, who had been watching him with an almost obscene
interest, saw him look up from the book and said, "Well?"

"I don't know." Paul shook his head. "It's damaging, I admit,
but I don't know what it's worth as proof. When you come right
down to it, he doesn't actually say anything that couldn't be part
of some boys' game, does he?"

"Doesn't say anything!"

Paul shook his head unhappily. "I don't know. He seems to
do everything that way. Impossible to pin down. Still . . ."

Laura gave him that same oddly smug look. "He wrote another
one after that," she whispered. "Just over there on the next page.
Read that one. He wrote it later last night, I guess. Just before
he went to bed or something. Go ahead, read it."

Paul turned the page and read:

December 25:

Everything changed. Lousy luck. Always figured my
mother's husband for masterpiece, but no time now. From
what she says, he must have heard Stu's silly oath about
Johnny Spence. Castrated father, cancer mother, and all the
rest. Teach me a lesson. Stay away from kid stuff. All right,

stepfather goes. Maybe premature, but a real pleasure.
Don't forget Stu and Laura, but stepfather first.

How? Time to think. If he didn't have guts to come
out with it when he heard it, won't have guts enough next
few days. Maybe could still be masterpiece? Matter of thinking. Must arrange so he knows. Imperative. Wouldn't want
to send loving stepfather off without saying good-bye. Exciting. Maybe good thing.

There was a heavy feeling at the pit of Paul's stomach, and
he was sure his new tic was showing. He said to Laura, "I'm going
to have a talk with Stu."

"Stu? Mr. Stuart?"

"That's right."

"Mr. Hamilton, I don't see any use talking to that boy. I
mean, you read what Mr. Robert wrote there, and——"

"All the same, I'm going to have a talk with Stu."

Laura sighed. "We just keep on wasting time and everything.
Well . . . can I talk to you some more after you finish with him?"

"I don't know. Yes, all right. Wait for me in the kitchen."

As he went through the doorway, out into the hall, Paul heard
Laura say, "I don't know what jails are for, if . . ."

Chapter 16

PAUL KNOCKED AT Stu's door and then opened it without waiting
for permission. It was a rudeness he regretted, but he wanted to
establish his adult authority, and he thought this was as good a
way as any. He went into the room and closed the door.

Stu was lying on the bed, doubled into a fetal sort of ball, looking more than half asleep. A comic book with a spaceship on its

cover lay on the floor beside the bed. He said, "Oh, hi, Mr. Hamilton. I guess I must have gone to sleep or something."

"I'm sorry to disturb you," Paul said, "but something very important has come up. There are some questions I have to ask you, Stu, and I want good straight answers."

Stu pushed himself up to a sitting position, resting his back against the bed's headboard. He had taken his shoes off, and his socks, inches too long for his feet, turned up at the ends. He looked like one of Disney's dwarfs. "Did I do something wrong, Mr. Hamilton?" he asked.

For some reason it annoyed Paul. "No, of course you didn't do anything wrong.

"Oh. Well, that's good. A guy don't always know. I mean, a kid don't always."

The annoyance drained out of Paul as suddenly as it had come— he had been subject to these abrupt changes lately, he thought— and was replaced by a surprisingly warm feeling of affection. "No, you didn't do anything wrong," he told Stu. "As a matter of fact, I've come to the conclusion that you're a pretty solid boy, and that's why I decided to ask you for help."

"Help? Well, gee whiz, Mr. Hamilton, I don't know if I can ——"

"Incidentally," Paul interrupted, "do you happen to know what time it is?" It was a cheap way to remind him. "I don't have my watch with me."

Stu grinned. He lifted his arm up dramatically to display his new watch. "Well, it says by my self-winding, waterproof, unbreakable watch . . . let's see, three-forty-seven and eleven— twelve—thirteen . . . the seconds are hard to catch up with."

"That's close enough. Mind if I sit down?"

"Sure, go ahead."

Paul sat on the bed beside Stu, although there were two chairs he might have chosen. "I have to talk to you about Robert," he said.

Stu gave him a sharp look. "Well . . . okay, I guess."

"I know you'd rather not answer questions about him, and to tell you the truth, I'd rather not have to ask them. But this is important, Stu. I mean that; this is honestly important. Do you understand?"

"I guess so." Stu nodded slowly, as if with effort. "Only I don't know if I can . . ."

"Our trouble is this, Stu: Robert is no ordinary boy. I'm sure you've noticed this yourself. And his mother and I can't always tell whether the unordinariness is a good thing or . . . or maybe a very bad thing. So we have to ask questions. We have no choice. You see that, don't you?"

"Well, I guess so," Stu answered uncomfortably. "The only thing is . . . well, okay."

"For example, I want to know how he gets along at school. I don't mean his marks or any of that; I know they're good enough. But how does he get along with the other boys? Does he have many friends?"

"Him and me are friends. Best friends, I guess."

"Yes, but you're a pretty tolerant kind of boy, Stu. Does he have many other friends?"

"As many as he wants, I guess. See, Bob's kind of funny. He don't want a lot of guys fussing around. It's like he don't need them. You know?"

"How about you? You have plenty of friends, I'll bet, don't you?"

Stu shrugged. "I get along with the guys okay." He grinned self-consciously. "Bob says it's because I'm as stupid as they are. You worried about Bob, like maybe he don't have enough friends or something?"

"That's part of it, maybe. Only part of it." Paul thought he could feel the whole thing bogging down, and he wondered if some cowardly corner of his mind were purposely skirting the real issue. "How about his teachers? Does he get along all right with them?" Even as he asked the question, he recognized it as another irrelevancy.

"Well, he makes good marks, like you said, except maybe in math. And he, you know, keeps his nose clean. Nobody's buddies with teachers. Not at Hastings, anyway."

Paul managed a smile. "No, I guess not. Well, then, let me ask you this. Does he have any enemies among the other boys?" This was more to the point, he thought. "I mean, real enemies?"

Stu looked up at him with narrowed eyes, as though trying to fathom his purpose. "None I know about," he said slowly. "Maybe Arny Bright or Stub Scofield, but nobody likes them very much. I got no enemies, so I guess neither has Bob."

"Doesn't necessarily follow," Paul said, to himself rather than to Stu. Then, "Does he get into many fights with the other boys?"

Stu chuckled. "Bob don't have to fight. That's for dopes like me, he says. I get in some fights sometimes, but Bob don't."

"Why is that?"

"Well, see . . ." Stu frowned. "Somebody makes a guy like me mad, and I just wade on in and get my nose bloodied. But Bob's smarter, I guess. Somebody does something to him, he just walks away and goes on up to his room and figures out something to do back. Something that fits, see what I mean. He don't just hit a guy to get even. He can think up better ways."

"What ways?"

"Oh." Stu's face went suddenly blank. "I can't think of any right now."

"Come on, Stu, what kind of things does he do to get even?"

Stu sat staring straight ahead, his face wooden.

"Now, listen, Stu, I don't want to have to . . . Stu, look at me."

Stu turned his face slightly upward toward Paul's, but he kept it totally expressionless; and his eyes focused, as if through Paul's head, at the wall behind him.

"Look," Paul said, "I told you this is important, but it's even more than that. It's . . . vital. Do you know what I mean by vital instead of important?"

"No, sir," Stu said flatly.

"I mean, it's so important, so vital, that kids keeping secrets from grownups . . . that doesn't go anymore. It's so serious that

—" Paul shifted his weight because he was beginning to feel a cramp in his left thigh. "You know the difference between sneaking some of the icing off a fresh cake and holding up the First National Bank? Now, do you understand what I'm trying to say?"

"No, sir." Stu squirmed over to the edge of the bed and threw himself off it with such violence that Paul thought he was going to pitch forward on his face. He retrieved his balance, and turning stiffly to face Paul, stood at a very formal military attention, looking at something distant over Paul's right shoulder. "Mr. Hamilton, if I've done anything wrong, you ask me about it and I'll tell you anything you want to know. But if it's Bob you want to know about . . . excuse me, sir, but I don't think you got any right to ask me. I think you ought to ask him."

He executed a smart left-face and would have marched right out of the room if Paul had not leaned forward, grasped him by the two shoulders and turned him back, forcing him to face the bed again. He got his feet comically entangled in turning, and although it didn't make Paul feel at all like laughing, something about the small mishap seemed to restore his position, which had tottered for a moment, as the dominant adult.

"Stu," he said, still holding the shoulders that felt padded with baby fat, "maybe I haven't made this as clear to you as I must. Because of something Robert has done, his mother and I are about to . . . we've been talking about me packing up and leaving. Because of Robert, Stu, and nothing else. I don't know if I can make you see how I feel about this, but it's very hard for a man to . . . it's a great loss. Does this mean anything to you, Stu?"

Stu bowed his head in an exaggerated way, making thick folds at the sides of his neck and under his chin. His voice was muffled. "I was around when my mother and father got separated."

"Oh. I'm sorry. Well, then, you have some idea, maybe, of what I'm trying to say."

"Yes, sir."

"So will you sit down and talk with me some more?"

"Yes, sir." Stu climbed up on the bed again and sat beside Paul, his feet dangling.

"Thank you," Paul said. He smoothed out a frown that had appeared without his consent. "This isn't very easy for me either, you know. Now. You said Robert had better ways than fighting to get even with the other boys. I want you to give me an example of that. Just so I'll get the picture."

Stu said, "Okay," but he looked unhappy. "Well, like the time Franky Crane told old man Engles about Bob cribbing on an algebra exam. Bob got hold of Franky's English Four notebook and took it down to the furnace room and burned it up. Franky pretty near flunked his midterm on account of it, and when we get back he won't get any Saturday liberties all January."

"Now, you say Robert got hold of Franky's notebook. How did he get it?"

"He just, you know, got hold of it."

"Did he go into Franky's room and steal it?"

Stu sighed. "Yes, sir. I . . . I caught him doing it."

"All right. Any more examples?"

"Well . . . just stuff like that. I can't think of anything else."

If Robert would go into a schoolmate's room to steal his notebook, then there was no reason to suppose that he wouldn't steal money from the handbag in Laura's room. But that, of course, was not what Paul was trying to find out. He looked down at Stu and felt some concern over what he was doing. He couldn't be sure what kind of trouble he was setting Stu up for.

"What would Robert do," he asked, "if he found out that you were talking to me like this?"

Stu made a fat grimace and said, "I don't know."

"He'd be angry, wouldn't he?"

"Oh, boy!" Stu took in a deep breath that wheezed like an old man's sigh. "You got a friend like Bob, you got to be careful all the time, let me tell you."

"Careful of what?" Paul pounced.

Stu looked up at him, surprised, and said mildly, "Careful, or he'll stop being friends with you."

"Would that make you so unhappy?"

"Well, sure."

"Why? I mean, why is it so important to you to be friends with Robert? Do you like him so much?"

Stu frowned down at his feet, dangling there just off the floor. "I like him all right," he said slowly and paused again, wrestling with an abstraction. "Only sort of like a grownup. You know? It makes me feel more like grown up myself, and not just a fat little kid, being friends with Bob. I don't know. I never thought about it before."

Not bad thinking for the first time around. "Tell me this. How did you happen to become friends in the first place, you and Robert?" It seemed an unnatural friendship to Paul, although he saw no advantage in saying so to Stu.

"Kind of funny thing. You know, I told you I saw him taking Franky Crane's English Four notebook out of his room? Well, I figured I was in for it good, because I didn't think Bob liked me much even before. But you know what? All of a sudden he started being friends with me. Just like that. A real funny thing, huh?"

"Yes." Paul thought it over for a time, liking it less and less. "Has he ever hurt you? Physically hurt you?"

Stu shook his head without speaking.

"Has he ever threatened to?"

"Not to really mean it."

"He keeps saying you talk too much. What is it he doesn't want you to talk about?"

At this, Stu began to look frightened again. "He's just like that, you know. He wouldn't want anybody to find out how many times he went to the bathroom yesterday. He just likes to keep things to himself."

"But he wouldn't make you swear such a terrible oath about that, would he, Stu? Your fingers and toes dropping off, your father castrated, your mother having cancer?"

The color drew back from the skin of Stu's face, leaving it pasty, like Laura's, and Paul wondered if anything was actually worth that. Stu said, "I think I have to go to the bathroom myself, Mr. Hamilton."

"What would Robert do to you if he thought you had told me about Johnny Spence?"

Stu bounced off the bed. Paul stood up more slowly, but in time to put himself between Stu and the door.

"I have to go, Mr. Hamilton," Stu said hoarsely. "I think I'm gonna be sick."

Paul said, "All right, be sick right here on the floor. I mean it, Stu. What we're talking about is more important." They stood where they were, facing each other, for a moment or two without speaking. Stu swallowed several times with difficulty, and Paul felt like a monster. He said, "I hate to do this to you, Stu. I ask you to believe I hate it. But I'm not going to let you go until we've talked this whole thing out. It's a hateful thing, but it's a thing that's happened to you and me because you're Robert's friend and I'm his stepfather. There had to come a day when we'd talk like this, just as surely as . . . as surely as it's after four o'clock now by your new watch." What a lousy thing, he thought. What a lousy thing, to bring the watch into it again. But he went on, "You might as well sit down again. I don't think you're really going to be sick. And you aren't going anywhere until we've got the thing all talked out."

Stu, who appeared to recognize authority when he saw and heard it, went back to the bed and half leaned against it instead of sitting down, as if he really did expect to be sick or to have to move in a hurry for some other reason. Paul sat beside him. The tic, unaccountably, had left his mouth.

"Let me tell you something," he said. "I don't know that it will help. It may just sound silly and sentimental to you, but I really mean it. It isn't just to get you to talk. If I could have had a son—and I'm sorry I never did—I would have been very pleased if he had turned out to be like you. A fat, comic-book-reading, honest kid. I don't know that it makes any sense to mention it right now."

"Yes, sir." Stu looked up at him shyly, wide-eyed and very solemn. "It makes sense to me."

"All right." Paul found that he had never been more embarrassed in his life, as if there were something dirty about it. It made him angry; whether with himself or with Stu or just with the unfortunate way things were, he couldn't be sure. "Then, let's get this over with. Did Robert kill Johnny Spence or didn't he?"

"What!"

"Oh, come off it, Stu. I heard the whole thing through the door the other night. The fingers and toes dropping off, the castration, the cancer, the whole thing. All to keep you from telling anybody that Robert killed Johnny Spence." Paul allowed a moment to pass while Stu stared up at him, his mouth hanging foolishly open. Then, "All right, did he or didn't he?"

"You mean, for real?"

"Is there another way to kill somebody?"

"You gotta be kidding! Bob wouldn't do a thing like that!"

"Then, how do you account for all that talk I heard? Swearing that terrible oath and all that?"

"Well, that's just part of . . . gee whiz, Mr. Hamilton, I'm not supposed to tell!"

"Well, right here is where you do, supposed to or not. Right here and right now!"

"Well, all that stuff . . . the oath and all that . . ." Stu swallowed with difficulty. "That's all just part of the game."

"Game?"

"Yeah, sure. I mean, yes, sir. Like any other game you make up when you're cooped up in a place like Hastings. You gotta do something, Mr. Hamilton. You'd go stir crazy if you didn't do something."

"You mean to say that's all there is to it? It's just a game?"

"Cross my heart, Mr. Hamilton." He crossed it. "Good gosh, Bob wouldn't do a thing like that!"

If it wasn't authentic sincerity, then Paul had to believe that Stu was an extraordinarily accomplished liar, and he didn't want to believe that. Still, if only because he would have liked the boy to be telling the truth, he knew he had to be doubly wary.

"It must be a very complicated sort of game," he said. "Tell me about it."

"Well . . ." Stu frowned. "It's like all make-believe. You know? It's no worse than reading murder mysteries, is it? Half my comic books are nothing but murder and, you know, holdups and that stuff. That's all there is to it."

Paul kept his voice stern. "How does it work?"

"I don't know if I can . . ." Stu sighed. "See, to begin with, something's got to happen. You can't just make something up all the way out of your own head. So something happens to somebody and you say you did it yourself, and then the other guy has to figure it all out. Okay?"

Paul shook his head. "Not very clear, I'm afraid, Stu. Maybe it would help if you took me through a little of it. Step by step. Do you know what I mean? Could you do that?"

"Cripes, Bob's gonna kill me!" Stu looked up at Paul, suddenly horrified. "I mean, he's gonna be awful sore. I didn't mean that other, like for real."

"I understand. Will you try to clear it up for me, though, this game of yours?"

"Well . . ." Stu gazed into a subjective distance for a moment and then turned back to Paul, looking unhappy but ready. "Well, like the time old Peggy Sewell—he teaches American history—like the time he had to go to Buffalo because his brother died. For real, I mean. So Bob said he kidnapped him, see? Peggy was gone and Bob said he kidnapped him, and then it was up to me to figure out how he did it and where he had old Peggy hid and how he was going to collect the ransom." He stopped, looked hopefully up at Paul, sighed again, and went on. "The cook at the Academy—an old lady named Mrs. Andrews; she's not there anymore—anyway, old Mrs. Andrews got out of bed in the middle of the night—she had a room up on the second floor, over the kitchen—and she fell downstairs and broke her hip. So I claimed I lured her out of bed and then pushed her. Bob had to figure out what I told her to get her out of bed in the middle of the night and how I got her to come to the head of the stairs so I could push her and stuff like that."

Paul just sat there waiting until Stu could endure the silence no longer.

"See, you have to write everything down in your diary," he said. "Before you claim you did it, you have to write down all about it. So you can't cheat, see?" And after another pause, "We got a real wild way of scoring. So many points for murder, so many for assault and for robbery—we had to make up a new one for kidnapping; we never had that one before—and what do you call it when you set fire to something? Arson. You get one point for thinking it up first, no matter what it is, and then the rest of the points—three or four or five—go to the other guy if he can figure it out in time, or to you if he can't. Okay?"

"All right. Now, tell me about Johnny Spence."

"Mr. Hamilton, are you gonna tell Bob about me, you know, shooting off my mouth like this?"

"I can't truthfully say yet, Stu," Paul told him. "I won't unless I have to."

"He won't ever be friends with me again, that's for sure."

"Maybe he won't have to know. Now, please tell me about this Johnny Spence."

Stu shook his head dismally. "Johnny's folks moved out west a while back. Around the first of December, I think it was. It was so far away that Johnny wasn't gonna be able to get home vacations and like that, so they took him out of the Academy. He was Bob's roommate. So he was gone, see, and Bob knew we probably never would see him again, so he said he killed him. For the game, you know."

Paul nodded. "How did he say he did it?"

"Well, I don't know yet. The Johnny Spence one's still going on, see. That's what I'm supposed to figure out—how he did it and where he hid the body and like that."

"Can you explain to me," Paul asked, "why, if this whole thing is just a little game, Robert threatened you the other night the way he did? Made you swear that nasty little oath?"

"That's part of it. No, honest, Mr. Hamilton. It's no good if you don't make like it was for real, is it? I know Bob's guilty, and as long as this game about Johnny Spence lasts, he's got to pretend he's worried about me talking. Don't you understand? What good would it be if it wasn't like for real?"

It began to make a kind of sense to Paul. He had to admit that there was more logic in crediting two thirteen-year-old kids with playing an elaborate game of make-believe, no matter how bloody, than there was in suspecting one of them of premeditated murder. Children, even odd children like Robert, just didn't murder people. Petty little misdemeanors, they might commit, yes, but murder was just too outlandish.

"It seems like a pretty gruesome game," he said to Stu.

"Well," Stu answered, "this morning I was reading in one of those comic books Bob gave me about a man that killed his business partner, and ground him up in a little hand meat grinder, and made a powder out of his bones by pounding two rocks together like the Indians used to make cornmeal, and then mixed the whole thing up and fed it a little bit at a time to his dog. That's a lot gruesomer than—Hey! You think maybe that could be what Bob did with Johnny?" He looked suddenly frightened again. "In the game, I mean, Mr. Hamilton."

Paul nodded and said, "I may be sick myself."

"Gee, I'm sorry, Mr. Hamilton, but you wanted me to——"

"All right. It's all right." Paul's eyes felt dried out, and the tic was back at the corner of his mouth. He put his fingertips to his eyes and pressed, rubbing slowly. He felt that he had no choice but to accept Stu's story. Actually, he wanted to accept it, even though it seemed to justify Elaine's asking him to leave her, even though it made him question his whole attitude toward Robert over the past two years. If Robert was not really a monster, after all, if he was just a growing boy with a somewhat exaggerated sense of the macabre, if he was just somebody who was able to command more of Elaine's affection than he, Paul, could get for himself, then wasn't he, as Elaine had said, a grown man, rather disgustingly jealous of a little boy? It was an unprepossessing picture. It made him, in spite of himself, ask himself who was the monster here, after all.

"Just one thing," he said to Stu. "If all this you've told me is true, then Johnny Spence is alive, isn't he?"

"Well, sure," Stu said. "Unless something happened to him since I saw him last, sure."

"Where did he move to? Out west, you said. Do you know where?"

"Seattle, I think. I didn't pay much attention. Hey, why don't you see if you can call him up long distance?"

"No," Paul said. "No, I think I believe you, Stu."

Stu stood up and smiled at Paul as though he had just received another gift of the magnitude of the self-winding watch. "Well, then, everything's gonna be okay, huh?"

Paul answered with something less than Stu's enthusiasm, "Yes, everything that matters to you."

"I mean, you won't have to tell Bob I shot my big fat mouth off now, will you?"

"No. No, I don't see any reason why I should."

"Gee, that's swell! Mr. Hamilton, I really do have to go to the bathroom. Not for sick, but, you know . . ."

"Sure, go ahead. I've finished with you."

Stu hurried to the door and opened it.

"Oh!" Laura said from out in the hall. "Excuse me. I was just looking for Mr. Hamilton."

"He's in there," Stu said and hurried away.

Laura came in and closed the door softly behind her. "Can we talk in here for a minute?"

Paul said, "Were you listening outside?"

Laura leaned toward him so far that, had she been only a little heavier, she must certainly have fallen forward. "You don't really believe what that boy said, do you, Mr. Hamilton?"

"Yes, I think I do."

"Well, I don't!"

"You have a right to believe whatever you like, of course. To me, what he said seems more logical than the other. They've simply been playing a little game."

"What about that diary?"

"Part of the game. You heard him."

"Then how about the money he stole from me? That makes it a pretty rough game, wouldn't you say?"

"That's another thing altogether," Paul said stiffly. "If you'll tell me how much you think he took, I'll write you a check for it."

Chapter 17

PAUL SPENT THE remainder of the afternoon prowling the house as if in search of something, disturbed because he had been wrong about Robert, disturbed because this disturbed him. When he realized that it was growing dark, he turned on all the lamps in the living room, trying to outnumber the gloom, and confined his pacing to the single room. The darkness deepened until night had fallen in earnest, and he began to worry because Elaine was late. Laura came into the room, looking sullen, and tried to question him about when she was expected to serve dinner, but he cut her short and sent her away. The telephone didn't ring, but he had lost interest in Al Dunlap and his researches in any case. What could Dunlap report?

He wondered what he would be expected to do now, what Elaine would expect. There was only one course open to him, really: admit to Elaine that he had been wrong about Robert—although he still believed a good psychiatrist wouldn't do the boy any harm —and then get out as fast as he could. Stu's story hadn't changed anything as far as Elaine was concerned, except to prove her right; there was nothing in it to make her change her mind about Paul's leaving. He kept looking around the room and reminding himself of such things as that the cost of reupholstering the couch was now no concern of his except perhaps at second hand, that he would shortly see the last of the library he disliked so heartily, that he would probably never again sit across the fireplace from Elaine, wondering how soon he could suggest going to bed without seeming lewd.

Through the front window he saw the car swing into the driveway. He could make out, in addition to the headlights, the silhouette of the station wagon against the background furnished by the snow. The car slithered a time or two and stopped. The lights went out. He realized suddenly, although he had been waiting for them so impatiently, that he wasn't ready to face Elaine and Robert. He hurried out into the hall and up the stairs. He heard the front door open just before he went into the bathroom. He heard Elaine laugh, and the sound was so gay it jarred him. He went into the bathroom and closed and, after a moment's hesitation, locked the door.

He turned on the harsh light and examined himself in the mirror. The tic at the corner of his mouth seemed to have gone away, but it had left a memory of itself in the muscles it had affected, a threat if not an outright promise to return. His face had a forbidding look that surprised him. He didn't feel stern; he felt sad and defeated. His chin and jaw and cheeks were beginning to darken faintly, but he thought he could get through the evening without another shave. His nose looked as if it had been oiled, and his hair needed combing. He put some cold water on his face and dabbed at it with a pink-flowered towel that he had always thought was foolishly feminine but wouldn't have to be concerned over any longer. He combed his hair, even brushed it a little, and tried to open the bathroom door, forgetting that he had locked it. He unlocked it, feeling silly, and went out.

Robert was sitting on the edge of one of the fireplace chairs. His profile had its usual controlled look, but there was something in the stiffness of his back, the almost braced attitude of his legs, that seemed to imply excitement. Elaine was standing beside the couch, facing Robert, and looking down at him as if it were the whole world she saw. Paul felt a recognizable twinge of jealousy.

Both Elaine and Robert had taken off their heavy coats, but their cheeks and noses were still rosy from the outdoor cold. Robert was ripping open the end of a long, narrow cardboard carton. His fingers were strong and almost indecently deft.

"Hello," Paul said. His voice sounded husky and weak, and only because of this, he added, putting more diaphragm into it, "Have a nice day?"

"Oh!" Elaine whirled about to face him with a more startled look than he thought was called for. It was as if she had forgotten his very existence. "Yes, a very nice day." She contrived a bad imitation of a smile. "Robert, why don't you run upstairs and unpack it? Show it to Stuart? Wouldn't that be nice?"

"I'll just get it out of the box and then take it up." Robert looked up at Paul, studied him, trying, or so it seemed to Paul, to read his mind. "How was your day?"

"I just loafed around," Paul told him. His mouth gave a warning twitch. "I didn't even get the phone call I was expecting. Haven't got it yet, at least."

"Did you and Stu have a nice little talk?"

Paul shrugged. "I stopped in to see him for a minute. How was the play?"

"We loved it," Elaine said. She was nervous. "We liked it very much, didn't we, Robert?"

"It was fine," Robert said. "Very good." He tugged at a stubborn strip of cardboard, frowning. "Of course, it was only fiction; plays are never quite the same as the real thing." He tore away the strip of cardboard angrily.

Paul smiled. The petulant gesture, tearing away the piece of cardboard, somehow made him feel better.

Elaine spoke as though she felt a need to make the noise rather than to communicate, "The most peculiar thing. Robert had it all figured out even before the first act ended. I mean it! He told me who the murderer was and how they would prove it and . . ." She looked at Paul as if daring him to belittle it. "He was right, too."

"All you have to do is keep your eyes open." Robert reached inside the carton and began tugging at something. "Every time the detective mentioned the gun, that blond girl with the fat legs looked at the fireplace. So that's where the gun was, and she was the one who put it there. And a lot of other things, too."

Elaine said, "She did have fat legs, didn't she?"

Robert smiled at her, and nodded, and at the same time pulled the blue-glinting barrel of a gun out of the carton.

"So you got your rifle," Paul said.

Robert pulled out the rest of the gun. "Springfield thirty." He put the stock to his shoulder and sighted down the slim barrel. The thing had a deadly look. "Old reliable. I won't stop any elephants with this thing, but it must be pretty good for people. It was standard army equipment for years." He tilted his head and looked up at Paul without taking the gun down from his shoulder. "One of my father's favorites, this was. He didn't want all the odds on his side."

"Could you tell what kind of a gun it was they were using in the play?" Paul asked him.

"It looked like a toy pistol to me." He took the rifle down from his shoulder and bent his head forward, studying what Paul took to be the loading mechanism. "I expect they wanted us to think it was a Luger."

"I'm interested in how you figured out who the murderer was," Paul said. "Is this a kind of hobby of yours? You read a lot of mysteries and that kind of thing?"

Robert, fingering the rifle, made a clicking noise that sounded ominous to Paul. "No, I don't care much for them," he said, as though talking to the gun.

"You don't?"

"Kid stuff." Robert turned the gun around and looked into the barrel with his left eye closed. "This thing needs cleaning."

Elaine said, "Well, why don't you take it upstairs and clean it, Robert?"

"All right." Robert stood up and moved toward the hallway, carrying the rifle as though ready to use it. "They've got some pretty silly laws in Nassau County, if you ask me, not firing harm-less little rifles. I'd like to try this thing out." He went a few steps into the hall and then came back and stood just inside the room, looking at Paul with a curious expression. "What made you ask me that? About mysteries?"

Paul shrugged. "Just conversation."

"What did you and Stu talk about this afternoon?"

Paul gave him what was meant to be a perfectly casual smile. "I asked him what time it was, and he told me."

Robert walked away thoughtfully.

Elaine waited until he had had time to reach the top of the stairs and then said to Paul, "What did that mean? What was that all about?"

"I don't know, exactly. He and Stu have some kind of secret going. Something to do with games. Elaine, there's something I want to tell you."

"Not any more of that, Paul," Elaine said. "I don't want to hear any more of it, and I won't listen to any more."

He looked at her and was aware, perhaps for the first time fully, of the magnitude of the loss he had sustained. It was not just that she was a beautiful woman, that the planes and surfaces, the texture and composition, were good. Thousands upon thousands of women were beautiful, and if it were no more than that, he could simply go out and find a replacement, as if for a used car or a worn-out suit. But for Elaine, there was no replacement. There was only one of her, and it just happened to be the one in all the world that was right for him. The thought of losing her made him feel sick, like being kicked in the solar plexus, if the soul had a solar plexus.

"No," Paul said quietly, "I don't mean to try to talk you into anything. I only wanted to tell you———"

"We've been over it and over it," she said, "and you know as well as I do that it will never come out right. Even if Robert hadn't found out . . ." Was she going to cry? Surely Elaine wasn't going to cry. "But since he did, I don't think there's any-thing more to . . ."

Out in the hall, the telephone rang.

". . . say about it." She turned away from him. She actually was in danger of crying. "There's somebody at the door."

"It's the telephone," he told her. He took the handkerchief out of his pocket—a clean handkerchief, luckily—and handed it to her. "Here. Just in case. I'll take care of the phone."

He turned away from her and walked through the opening into the hallway, feeling, not very charitably, glad that she too had been kicked in the solar plexus. Laura appeared in the kitchen doorway, on her way to the telephone, but he waved her back. He took up the phone, and ignoring the chair that was meant to be sat on while phoning, said, "Hello," in a tone that surprised him because it sounded angry.

"I'd like to speak to Mr. Paul Hamilton, please. This is Al Dunlap calling."

"Oh." Paul craned his neck to peer back into the living room. Elaine was facing away from him, not using his handkerchief. "Yes," Paul said softly into the telephone, "this is Paul Hamilton."

"Sorry I didn't get to you sooner, Mr. Hamilton. It took a while, checking everything out."

"That's all right. Actually, I seem to have found out what I wanted to know myself."

"*You* found out!"

"I seem to have, yes."

Elaine came through the opening, walking with quick little steps that would have clicked authoritatively on a hard surface. As she passed Paul, she tucked the handkerchief, quite dry, into his shirt pocket. She climbed firmly up the stairway, holding her head high, needing nothing from anybody.

"Well," Dunlap said unhappily at the other end of the line, "I can't help what happened in between. I did the job you hired me for, Mr. Hamilton, and I've been put to some trouble doing it. I feel I've earned my fee, even if——"

"Oh, no question about that," Paul assured him. "I'll get a check in the mail first thing in the morning, if you'll just give me the final figure."

"Oh, I'm sorry. I thought for a minute you meant——"

"No, no, not at all."

"Well, now, look," Dunlap said, "wouldn't it be just as good if I came out to your place tomorrow and picked the check up?"

Paul hesitated. He couldn't think, just at the moment, how making an appointment for tomorrow morning would affect his wavering position in the household. "Why, I suppose so, yes, if you really feel——"

"Tell you the truth, I could use the money soonest possible. You know how that goes. And anyway . . ." Dunlap's voice turned oddly funereal. "Anyway, I want to get this report off my hands. I mean, I want to be finished with it."

"What's that supposed to mean?" Paul asked him. "If you want to make your report, why don't you just go ahead and make it? What's wrong with right now?"

"No, sir, I'm afraid not. Not on the telephone."

"But from what I understand, there's really no——"

"I don't know anything about what you understand, Mr. Hamilton. As soon as I finish talking to you here, I'm going to type out a full report. I'll bring it out to you first thing in the morning. If I get like a ten or ten-thirty train, will that be okay? I want to deliver the report by hand, pick up my check, and that's the end of it for me. If I get in Great Neck, say, around half past eleven, is that okay?"

"All right, if you think that's the best way," Paul said. "I wouldn't make it any later than that, though. I . . . I may not be here after noon. I don't want you to give that report to anybody else."

Paul put the phone back in its cradle and climbed the stairs, going back over the conversation. He didn't actually know Al Dunlap, he reminded himself. Maybe the man was given to working up his own little intrigues, just to make his function seem more significant—to himself as well as to his clients. Maybe he played some little games himself.

Feeling foolish, Paul knocked at the door of the bedroom he had shared with Elaine for two years.

There was an ambiguous thumping sound from inside, and Elaine said, "Robert?"

"No, it's Paul."

"Oh." A silence and then, "You can't come in now, Paul."

He was overtaken by another of the surges of sudden anger that seemed to have become habitual with him lately. "I don't want to come in," he shouted. "I just want to let you know, I've made an appointment for tomorrow morning. I have to be here for it. As soon as it's over, I'll pack up and get the hell out."

"Paul!"

"And a good thing for everybody!"

Elaine opened the door. "I'm sorry, Paul. Of course you can come in."

Chapter 18

THE GROVE AT night was a place of deceptive shadows that moved now with the low wind, and now, seemingly, against it, of their own volition. The light, sickly from an aging moon, was given back by the snow with scarcely any loss of candlepower but with total loss of even its original puny pretense of warmth. The shadows, surprisingly sharp against their white background, not only moved irrationally but also were irrational in themselves, since the light, seeming to emanate equally from the moon and the snow, ought to have been working as much against them as for them. The only sound, except for the occasional snapping of a twig frozen beyond endurance, was the squeak of shoes on dry snow.

"Judas," Stu whispered, "how can you see where you're going? This place is spooky."

"I was born here," Robert said in a soft voice that was less penetrating than Stu's whisper. "I know where I'm going without seeing. Now, shut up until we get farther from the house."

They moved on through the grove, Stu doing his best to follow Robert, until they came to the clearing, the spot farthest removed from the house within the confines of the property. The light here was less harassed by shadows than under the trees, but it was no less pale or wintry. The snow lay on the ground like a clean sheet, innocent of tracks.

A few paces into the clearing, Robert turned about and stopped Stu in his tracks simply by facing him. "All right, now you can talk. Nobody's going to hear us out here."

Stu made a puzzled face in the dim light and said, "Who was gonna hear us up in your room where it was warm? I'm cold."

"Who heard us the first night we were up there? The night we got here?"

There was a short pause before Stu answered. "The night we got here? How should I know?"

"You talked to What's-his-name today, didn't you? My mother's husband." Robert seemed to move in closer to Stu without actually taking a step in his direction at all. "Didn't you?"

"Well, sure. We were all by ourselves in the house, except for that Laura. Sure, we talked a little bit."

"And what did you talk *about,* a little bit?"

"Well, you know, like . . . like watches and comic books. Oh, and how he always wanted a son—until he got one, of course, when he married your mother. And . . . you know, like that."

"And about games?"

"You always think I spill my guts, every chance I get."

"What did you tell him?"

Stu looked up into Robert's face stubbornly and said nothing. "What did you tell him, Stu?"

Stu lowered his head and mumbled, "I shoulda stayed up at the Academy. Some Christmas!"

Robert studied him with a calculating expression for a time and then made a light, laughing sound. "I've just had a great idea.

I wish I'd had the time to put it down in my book. Maybe I will, later on."

"Yeah?" Stu looked up at the taller boy without much hope. "So let's go back and do it. I'm cold. My gloves ain't even in my pocket. I haven't even got any gloves."

Robert said, "Do you know how cold it is?"

"Too cold for me."

"Nine degrees above zero, the radio said at eleven o'clock. That's twenty-three degrees below freezing. Now, bundled up the way we are, I expect we could keep from freezing to death out here for . . . I don't know, a good long while. Overnight, anyway. But what do you suppose would happen if we took all our clothes off? Stripped down to, say, our shorts? How long do you think we'd last that way?"

Stu shivered. "You're making me colder than ever."

"A couple of hours." Robert nodded, sure of himself. "That's about all, I figure, about a couple of hours. Maybe a little more, maybe a little less, but that's pretty close. If we started now, let's say, you ought to be dead by two o'clock. Three o'clock at the outside."

"Me!"

"Who else? You didn't think I was going to do it, did you?"

"Aw, come off it, Bob!"

"Aw, come off it, Bob," Robert mimicked. "What did you tell him? How much did you spill to him?"

Stu waggled his head at Robert. "Why do you always have to think I'm gonna . . ."

"Okay, then!"

Robert reached out both his hands and took one of Stu's shoulders in each of them. He spun Stu around, switching hands, so that they were both facing in the same direction, toward the house, Robert behind Stu. He released Stu's shoulder with his right hand, grasped his chin with it, and twisted his head around so that his chin almost touched his right shoulder.

"Keep your mouth shut!" he said tautly. "Just one more little twist . . ." he demonstrated, ". . . and your neck cracks. Okay?

No yelling, or that's what happens. Now." He released Stu's left shoulder carefully and with his left hand began unbuttoning Stu's sheepskin parka.

"Hey, cut it out!" Stu managed to croak, but very softly. His voice had a strangled sound. "Cut it out, will you!"

"Shut up." Robert gave Stu's neck a suggestive little jerk. "You know what I mean?"

"Okay, okay."

Working very slowly and cautiously, Robert slipped Stu's parka off his left shoulder first, pulling the arm back painfully, and then, running his free hand across Stu's back in order to keep the pressure against his neck constant, flipped the coat off his right shoulder. It slid down the arm, hesitated for a moment over the right hand, and then dropped off the arm into the snow. Robert kicked it out of the way.

Stu whispered, "Come on, will you? It's cold."

Robert said, "It's going to get a lot colder. Now, how much did you tell him?"

"For Pete's sake! We talked about my new watch and the comic books and . . ."

"All right!"

Robert began unbuttoning the heavy, shapeless sweater Stu had been wearing under the parka. "I didn't finish about this idea I have," he said. "When I've got you stripped down to your shorts, I make you lie down on your face in the snow. You won't yell if I tell you not to; you haven't got the guts. Actually, I don't so much as put a hand on you. I just make you lie there and freeze to death." By this time Robert had the sweater hanging on Stu's right shoulder. He slipped it off, as he had done with the parka, but it stuck at the elbow. He reached down between himself and Stu and quickly jerked it off and threw it into the snow. "What did you tell him?"

Stu said, his voice quiet with disbelief, "Hey, you know, this ain't nothing but a little old cotton shirt. A guy could get pneumonia or something."

"Pneumonia doesn't mean a thing to a corpse. What did you say to him?"

"I told you, I just . . ."

"All right!" Robert gave Stu's neck a nasty little twist and went to work on his shirt. It was buttoned up to the top, but there was no tie to get in Robert's way. "By two o'clock—or by three at the latest, as I said—you'll be dead. It isn't such a bad death, Stu. Once you get past the pain, it's just like going to sleep. At least, that's what they say. So, at two o'clock, you're dead. I take you and your clothes back into the house without anybody seeing me. It won't be easy with all that blubber you carry around, but I can do it. So, I put your clothes away where they belong, and I dress your body in pajamas and tuck you into bed as lovingly as your own mother would. Even more lovingly, maybe." He had the shirt unbuttoned and was pulling the tail out from beneath Stu's corduroy trousers. "Can you imagine what happens in the morning? They find you lying there in bed in your pajamas, dead as a mackerel, but all thawed out. Who can tell you froze to death? You must have had a heart attack. Or something that medical science never heard of yet. Who knows?"

"They'd find dirt and snow and stuff on my clothes," Stu said.

"You know, you're right," Robert said, mock-admiringly. "We'll have to clean them up, won't we?" He didn't bother to ease the shirt off but jerked it straight down, holding the collar, ripping it at both shoulders. "So, what was it you told my mother's husband? Can you remember now?"

"Okay," Stu said. "Okay, I'll tell you."

"Do that," Robert said, "while I'm taking your pants off." He began fumbling with Stu's belt buckle. "And don't try to lie to me; you'll never get away with it."

"Well, let me get my neck straightened out, will you? I can't hardly talk at all this way." And after Robert had released only a little of the pressure on his neck, "I had to tell him about the game."

"You little bastard!"

"Well, I couldn't help it! He made me!"

"Keep your voice down."

"You shouldn't ever have brought me here."

"How much about the game?"

"Well, about old Peggy Sewell and Mrs. Andrews and . . . and Johnny Spence."

"Oh?" Robert paused just before unzipping Stu's trousers. "That was bright of you, wasn't it? What about Johnny Spence? How much about him?"

"I said he moved to Seattle; what else? Bob, can I put my stuff back on? I'm freezing."

Robert said, "I ought to go ahead and finish this."

"You can have the points," Stu told him. "Honest. I'm gonna catch pneumonia or something."

"All right." Robert pushed Stu away from him hard enough to throw him down on his hands and knees in the snow. "Not that I care whether you get pneumonia or not. Get your things on. We've got to get back into the house before they miss us."

"Okay, okay, okay." Stu, still on his knees, was gathering up his clothes. "You didn't have to tear my shirt."

"Oh, shut up."

Chapter **19**

ELAINE WAS GONE when Paul woke up. Her bed had been made and the whole room straightened up, so that the only messy thing in it was his own tousled bed. He stood up and stretched his back, which ached as though from a day of hard labor. Well, was anybody going to tell him that yesterday had been an easy day?

He was on his way to the bathroom when he noticed the note on the top of his dresser, leaning against the box he kept his cuff links in. He picked it up and read, in Elaine's large, careful hand:

Dear Paul:

Since you didn't seem to want to talk last night, I decided to wait until this morning and leave you this.

I assume that, since you have this appointment or whatever it is today, we won't be going up to Vermont for the skiing. We'll obviously have to put that off for another day. Robert is very disappointed. I only hope the snow holds.

We probably couldn't have gone anyway, because Stuart isn't feeling at all well this morning. He seems to have got the sniffles and is running a temperature. I don't think it's so bad we need to have Dr. Strong in, but I've told him to stay in bed and covered up. I gave him one of those antihistamine pills that work so well for Robert, and I'm sure he'll be all right.

Robert and I have decided to take a drive out toward Montauk Point. Not all the way, of course, but as far as we can get by lunchtime and then back. We'll be home in plenty of time for dinner. I know you said something about leaving right after your appointment, but I'm sure you'd forgotten all about the skiing when you said that.

I've told Laura to bring Stuart's lunch up to him and to give him more antihistamine pills every four hours, but you might just check on her to make sure she doesn't forget.

We'll be back in plenty of time for dinner.

Love,
Elaine.

She was having the same trouble he was having, Paul could tell. She didn't know what attitude to take toward this new relationship of theirs. She didn't know how casual to be or whether or not to avoid reference to small marital intimacies. It was a sad little note. Paul dropped it on his bed and went into the bathroom.

From the mirror, he looked back at himself out of ravished eyes. The bags under them seemed to have darkened a great deal since yesterday, and the corners were blood-red. With the white lather on his face, they seemed to turn even darker and to shrink back into his head. Nonsense. It was also nonsense, although he felt that way, to feel that the house had turned against him. In the first place, had it ever seemed to be for him? Besides, houses were made of wood, plaster, bricks, steel, and things of that sort. They did not have the equipment for being pro- or anti-anybody. Still, nonsense or not, the house made him uncomfortable this morning. He shaved too quickly and nicked his chin. The corner of his mouth where yesterday's tic had been felt tender but held still while he shaved over it.

Without knowing precisely why, he began dressing in outdoor things—a wool shirt, a lined windbreaker, heavy shoes. A walk in the snow before breakfast, he decided. It might give him some appetite for breakfast, because he certainly had none now.

He took his fleece-lined overcoat and his heavy galoshes out of the misshapen closet under the stairway and put them on. He heard Laura making dishwashing noises in the kitchen and knew he ought to give her some idea of when he would like to have his breakfast, but he decided not to, since he didn't know himself. He went out the front door quietly, thinking perhaps she wouldn't notice that he had come downstairs.

His first breath of the icy outdoor air made him cough, not unpleasantly. He closed the door snugly behind him, wondering how many more times he would do that. He made his way down the unswept front steps—let Robert clean them off—slowly and very cautiously, like an old man aware that his bones were turning brittle. He decided not to take the driveway, which, except for the lonely-looking ruts the station wagon had made yesterday and this morning, bore as virgin a burden of snow as the lawn itself. He turned to his right at the bottom of the steps and made his way, lifting his feet high, around the other side of the house back toward the grove.

Behind the house he found two sets of tracks in the otherwise unspoiled snow, each made by two pairs of feet, one leading into the grove and the other out of it and back to the library door.

It was clear without even a close examination that the tracks had been made by Robert and Stu—the long, narrow shoe and the thick, stubby one. Paul stood for a time, considering the wisdom of following the trail back into the grove. He couldn't do it without leaving his own tracks, of course, and this would advertise to Robert that he had been investigating; but he couldn't put his finger on any real harm this would do, and there was always a chance of learning something. He started back toward the grove, walking beside the outgoing set of tracks, making no attempt to disguise the trail he was leaving himself.

It became clear at once that the boys had gone right on through the grove to the clearing at the far corner. The tracks must have been made in darkness. The long, narrow shoes seemed to have moved firmly enough and with assurance; but the stubby marks left by Stu were less widely separated, even overlapping in places, and twice turning sharply at the very base of a tree trunk. It made Paul smile, although somewhat grimly. He could picture Stu, trying to follow at the pace Robert set for him, tripping over his own feet, walking into trees, complaining mildly. Stu was a boy who enjoyed his comfort. He would hardly have undertaken such a walk in the dark without considerable pressure from Robert. And Robert would never have put himself to so much trouble without a good solid purpose.

The snow just inside the clearing was badly trampled and told Paul little except that the two boys had done a good deal of moving around in a small space. As if they had been fighting? It wouldn't have been much of a fight, Paul had to admit; Stu simply was not equipped either physically or emotionally to stand against Robert for any length of time with any success.

In the snow a little apart from the heavily trampled area Paul noticed several handprints, as if one of the boys had spent some time on his hands and knees. That would be Stu, of course, not only because the prints were short and thick but also because it was impossible to imagine Robert in such an undignified position, for any reason, under any compulsion. There were two shapeless depressions in the snow near the handprints, both of them too shallow and too vaguely outlined to tell Paul anything. He wondered what Al Dunlap, the professional at this kind of thing, would have made of them.

As if the thought had conjured up the original, Paul heard the slamming of an automobile door, probably in the driveway. Without any very good reason, he felt quite sure that it was Dunlap, even though he had not expected the detective until much later. He turned back toward the house and half ran through the trees because he had a sudden, not very clearly understood dread of having Dunlap ushered into the house. Elaine and Robert were not in there, of course, but he still felt that way. He followed his old tracks until he was out of the grove and then veered away from them toward the driveway.

A man in a hat and overcoat conspicuously made for city rather than country wear was walking with what jauntiness he could contrive up the driveway toward the garage, keeping to the ruts the station wagon had made and slipping precariously at every third or fourth step. Paul waved to him and he waved back, half falling at the same time, as if the gesture had overbalanced him. Paul slowed down to a fast walk and continued along the driveway toward the man. He could see now that it was Al Dunlap.

Before they had quite met, the detective called, "Cabdriver was scared to come up into the driveway. Got stuck up here once, he claimed."

"Yes, that would be Denny Perkins. He's not very good on snowy roads, I'm afraid."

"Pretty good at picking up a buck. He's charging me two dollars just to sit out there and wait."

Paul grinned, pulled off his heavy right glove, and shook hands with Dunlap. "I didn't expect you until around eleven."

"Got the eight-forty-two," Dunlap said. "Couldn't seem to sleep, somehow."

Paul looked down at Dunlap's feet and said, "As long as you've worn your overshoes, would you mind just walking around out here while we talk?" He didn't feel like going in the house yet. "Instead of going inside? Are you too cold?"

Dunlap looked mildly surprised but said, "No, it was warm in the cab. I don't mind cold weather too much." He turned his head slowly from left to right, scanning the snowy landscape. "It's all slush in the city this morning. Sure looks prettier this way. I can't seem to stand up on it though."

"We're not on level ground here," Paul told him. "You'll be all right around back of the house."

While they walked together slowly back toward the grove, puffing little clouds of misty breath, Dunlap wriggled his left hand down through his tightly wrapped muffler and into a mysterious recess inside his coat. "Got the report right here," he said. He struggled for a time with some hidden obstruction and then pulled out a fat envelope. "Worked until 'way past midnight on this thing. Kind of touchy."

"Touchy?" Paul took the envelope but frowned down at the shorter man. "I can't see why, if this boy is well and happy and living with his parents out in Seattle."

Dunlap's face went quite blank, as if, after all, the cold which he didn't mind too much had frozen it stiff. "Is that the way you heard it?"

"Why, yes."

They had left the driveway and were now just at the corner of the house, walking slowly back toward the grove. Dunlap stopped and faced Paul, who was forced to stop, too. "The kid doesn't live in Seattle, Mr. Hamilton," Dunlap said tonelessly. "Fact is, he doesn't live anywhere anymore."

"I don't understand."

"He died last November twenty-eighth, approximately three-thirty P.M., on the premises of Hastings Military Academy. John R. Spence, Wheeling, West Virginia, age thirteen, eyes——"

"No, no," Paul said. He shook his head at Dunlap. "You must have the wrong Johnny Spence. This one moved with his parents to Seattle a few weeks ago."

Dunlap blinked his eyes once, slowly. "Only John Spence they ever had at Hastings. I checked. Last November twenty-eighth, the swimming coach—football, basketball, and squash, too—found

John R. Spence, from Wheeling, West Virginia, at the bottom of the new indoor pool with his head cracked open."

"An . . . accident?"

Dunlap shook his head deliberately. "I don't think so, no. There wasn't any water in the lungs at all. The way I figure, if a kid dives too deep, like the school officials said, and cracks his skull on the bottom, he still breathes anyway a couple of times, gets some water in his lungs, and he gets the crack on the front of his head or on the top, most likely, not in the back." Dunlap shook his head again despondently. "This kid was conked and thrown into the pool, already dead."

"But if it wasn't in the newspapers or anything, then I don't really see——"

"Don't mean a thing."

"There must have been an inquest."

"Private. I'll tell you how it was, Mr. Hamilton. They didn't give out to anybody that the kid was dead. Not only the school officials but the local cops, too, wanted it that way. They got the state to go along. Kind of sneaky, maybe, and the press is gonna tear them apart when it finally gets out, but they figure they got a better chance of pinning it on the boy that did it this way."

"Boy?"

"Boy. One of the kids at the Academy. Got to be that way. The way they figure is, let the kid think he got away with it and maybe he'll show himself some way. I don't buy it, because maybe the way he'll show himself is by knocking off another kid, but that's the way they figure. No, the boy was murdered, Mr. Hamilton. I aim to take my check from you, but I wish I'd never got mixed up in this. I don't like murder. I don't even like divorces, but they got it all over murder."

"I still don't see why it couldn't have been accidental."

"It was murder, Mr. Hamilton. You take it or leave it, whichever way you can stomach it, but it was murder. They're still working on it, the locals and the state people are. I had a long talk with the superintendent of the Academy. He found out who this young Spence had been seen with the afternoon he died.

Three kids. It's all in the report. Bates, Reagan, and Scofield. One of them was his roommate; I forget which." Dunlap gave Paul a long, searching look, and his expression softened somewhat. "Mr. Hamilton, you hire a detective to check on something because you want to know the truth. When he gets it for you, you can't be sore at him because you don't like it. If you hadn't suspected something like this, you never would have come to me in the first place, would you?"

"No, that's true. Well . . . if you'll come in the house with me now, I'll make out your check."

Dunlap didn't seem to hear him. He turned completely around, studying the house and grounds with a peculiarly cynical look. "Nice place you got here, Mr. Hamilton."

"Thank you."

"A man doesn't get married, he never has anything like this. Who the hell needs a big house in the country when he's got no wife or kids or anything? Same time, you have to stop and think when you see a nice place like this. You got a couple of boys around, haven't you?"

"What makes you think that?"

Dunlap smiled modestly. "Tracks in the snow over there." He pointed. "Too little for a man, wrong shape for a woman or a girl. Couple of boys, it's gotta be. Yours?"

"My wife's son and a friend of his."

"Home for the holidays?"

Paul nodded.

"From Hastings?" And when Paul didn't answer, "Look, Mr. Hamilton, I hate to be nosy when I'm not getting paid for it, but there's something I feel like I have to say to you. When you get mixed up in a homicide case, there's only one way to do it. You gotta do it by the book."

"I don't know what you're talking about."

"No," Dunlap said quietly. "Well, I'll just go ahead and finish, anyway. Okay?"

Paul shrugged.

"If a man knows somebody that's guilty of murder or even might be, he's a damn fool if he keeps his mouth shut about it. I don't mean just because he's setting himself up for an accessory rap; I mean more like morally he's got a duty. The way I see it, a man—or a boy, Mr. Hamilton—has got to be wrong in his mind somehow before he gets to the point of killing somebody, I don't care how much pressure he's under. You know what I mean? It's abnormal to kill people, and normal people don't do it. What I mean to say is, if you're keeping your mouth shut about somebody that killed once, you're just leaving the guy free to kill again. You're not doing anybody any favors, least of all the killer. He's sick, the killer is, and he won't get well as long as you leave him running around loose. If it's somebody close to you, why, all the more reason. Do you understand what I'm trying to say, Mr. Hamilton?"

"The only thing I understand is that none of this has anything to do with me."

Dunlap sighed. "Jesus, Mr. Hamilton, I couldn't sleep all last night myself; and what have I got to do with it? I'm just the hired help, doing like I'm told. But I couldn't sleep because I know damn well there's a kid walking around somewhere that kills other kids. I don't know who it is, and I'm just as glad. But if I can't sleep, I sure don't see how you're going to be able to. Mr. Hamilton, do you know who the kid is?"

"If you'll come inside," Paul said, very formally, "I'll give you your check. I don't believe you have any further responsibility in this matter."

Dunlap smiled at him. "I wish I could believe it like that. I sure as hell wish I could make it that simple for myself." He sighed so deeply that the cold air made him cough. "Okay, let's go in the house and settle up. If I came out here for anything besides that, I guess I wasted my time."

Paul led the way around the house, feeling sick—and he knew it—from the effort of deluding himself. He said, "Thank you," over his shoulder because he felt he owed Dunlap something for the lecture.

Dunlap caught up with him. "One more thing," he said. Paul shook his head. "Nothing more, please. That's all."

"Yes, just this one thing." They stopped. At least get it finished out here, Paul thought. Don't let him bring it into the house. Dunlap frowned and seemed to be thinking along more complicated lines that he found comfortable. "Something maybe you don't know, Mr. Hamilton. Maybe you're thinking about handcuffs, and bread and water, and solitary confinement, and—you know—police brutality, and that kind of stuff." He shook his head. "They don't have any of that anymore. Not these days. Not with kids, that's for damn sure. A kid goes in—a sick kid like this one we're talking about—and the first thing they think about is, how can they help him. No, it's true. If I had a kid, he was in a jam like this, the first place I'd want to take him would be to the cops. Not just to get him off my hands, but to do the best by him I could. They got people trained to handle mixed-up kids. They got the best psychiatrists in the business, and if you're thinking anything else, then you . . . well, okay. You got to do it your way, I can see that. So let's go settle up."

And what was going to happen to Elaine? Paul thought. None of Al Dunlap's preaching said anything about that. What in God's name was going to happen to Elaine?

Chapter 20

PAUL STOOD AT the wide front window and watched Al Dunlap's fight to keep his feet under him on the way back to his cab. He would never see Al Dunlap again, he felt sure, and he thought it was a shame, because Dunlap was a good man. They might have been good friends if Dunlap had been an educator or a next-door neighbor or if they had met in any way not connected with this monstrous thing that had happened. If it actually had happened.

He turned away from the window and for a moment felt dizzy. He needed some breakfast, he told himself. Among a host of other things, he needed some breakfast. He crossed the living room, the hall, and the dining room, still feeling somewhat off balance, and went into the kitchen. Laura very nearly dropped a plate she was drying.

"I'm sorry," Paul said. "I didn't mean to startle you. Do you think I could have some toast and coffee or something?"

"I could fix you some bacon and eggs if you want." She still sounded sullen. "I fixed some for Mrs. Hamilton and Mr. Robert, so I guess I can fix some for you."

"Thanks, Laura, but toast and coffee will be fine. Especially coffee."

"I just made some fresh for me, but there's plenty. You want a cup now, while I make the toast?"

He nodded and then said, "Yes, please."

"They went out for all day, I guess. Mrs. Hamilton and Mr. Robert. She just said they'd be back for dinner."

"I know. She left me a note."

"Mr. Stuart's got the sniffles or something. He's up in the guest room. I have to give him pills and take his lunch up to him." She filled one of the gray cups with beautiful steaming coffee. "It don't surprise me a bit that boy's got the sniffles. Where do you want me to serve your coffee, Mr. Hamilton?"

"Right here." Paul sank down into one of the metal kitchen chairs. "What do you mean, you're not surprised?"

"They were out in the grove 'way late last night, him and Mr. Robert." She set the coffee down in front of Paul. "I got something to tell you, Mr. Hamilton."

Paul tasted the coffee. It burned his tongue, but he thought it was going to be very good for his soul. "Do you think it could wait until I've had a little coffee, Laura? Whatever it is you want to tell me? I've heard quite a lot already this morning."

"From that man that was out in back with you?" Laura had taken a half-used loaf of round pumpernickel out of the breadbox, and she leaned forward toward Paul now, holding the loaf in her two hands, as if ready to pass it to him like a basketball. "I saw you both out there, talking and talking, and he gave you something in an envelope. Mr. Hamilton, was he a policeman?"

Paul said, "If you're going to make some toast out of that bread, Laura, will you please do it? I'm afraid the business that man and I were discussing was private."

Laura turned away, remembering to be sullen. "It's not like I'm just snooping, Mr. Hamilton. I've got a right to know what's going on. I've been threatened."

"Let me have the toast first, will you, please, Laura? After that we can talk."

"Well . . ." She cut a slice off the loaf of bread expertly. "Well, okay."

He watched Laura make the toast, watched the sharp joints and the angular movements and marveled that she held together at all. It was a foolish thing to be thinking about just now, of course. What he had to think about was what Al Dunlap had told him and what it was going to do to him. To everybody. It made a liar of Stu. It made a murderer of Robert. It justified—more than justified—his own feelings about Robert. What it was going to do to Elaine, God alone knew. If it was true.

Laura brought him his toast and looked at him pleadingly. He pretended not to see the look. He took a bite of the toast, and it tasted like sawdust mixed with butter. The trouble was with his palate, he knew; ordinarily he was very found of pumpernickel toast. He decided that he had better eat it, no matter how it tasted. An empty stomach wasn't going to help him get through the day.

He had taken Dunlap's report out of its envelope, folded it twice carefully, and stuffed it into the pocket of his fleece-lined overcoat, which was now hanging again in the stairway closet. He didn't know where to hide it properly. His little study off the bedroom was too obvious; it was where anyone—Robert, for example—would look. He was going to have to carry it around in his pockets, he supposed. Until it was no longer a secret document.

He hadn't been able to make himself read the report, but he knew, of course, that he must, sooner or later. He was almost able to smile. He must read the report, if only to avoid wasting all that money he had paid to Al Dunlap. It couldn't hurt to read it, anyway, really. He was already pretty well convinced.

He pushed his plate aside with one piece of toast untouched. He said to Laura, "Now I'd like another cup of coffee, please. I'll listen to whatever it is you want to tell me while I'm drinking it."

"Okay." She poured the coffee and stood holding the pot, as if ready to pour more. "I haven't been sleeping very good, nights lately."

"I'm not surprised. Why don't you have a cup of coffee yourself, Laura? And sit down?"

"Thank you." She poured a cup of coffee for herself but stood beside the sink to drink it. She made a gurgling sound that Paul found extremely distasteful. "So I was awake last night when Mr. Robert and Mr. Stuart got up and sneaked out of the house. They went out to the grove in back."

"I saw their footprints," Paul told her.

Laura nodded. "I sneaked out, too."

"*You* did!"

"After them. Well, I was scared to do it, but I was scared anyway, wasn't I? So I put on my . . . I put some things on and my heavy coat and I went out after them."

"I didn't see your footprints."

She gave him her smug look. "I went out the library door to the driveway and walked in the tire tracks down as far as the garage. From there I went on over to the grove. You could see those tracks, if you want to look."

Paul shook his head. "What happened?"

"Well, I didn't get as close as I wanted to because I was just too scared. I couldn't see them hardly at all, but I could hear part of what they said. Just words sometimes. I think Mr. Robert was taking Mr. Stuart's clothes off or something."

"What!"

"Well, that's what it sounded like to me. Mr. Stuart said, 'Hey, I got nothing on but a little old cotton shirt.' Something like that. And I heard cloth ripping, too. You know, there's nothing else sounds like that."

"But why in the name of heaven would he want to take the boy's clothes off?"

Laura blushed.

"Oh, come on, Laura!"

"And Mr. Robert said—and I heard this part real plain; the way the wind was blowing or something, I guess—he said, 'So you'll be dead by two o'clock, or anyway three.' Now, I heard that with my own two ears, Mr. Hamilton."

"Well, he wasn't dead at two o'clock, was he? Or three."

Laura looked angry. "No, but he's upstairs in bed, sick. What about that? Anyway, maybe Mr. Robert meant two or three o'clock this afternoon. You think he poisoned him or something?"

"No, I don't think he poisoned him, Laura. And I wish you'd stop imagining things." Paul could feel the tic making a fresh start at the corner of his mouth. He wished he could be as sure as he sounded that Laura was imagining things. When you came right down to it, why did poison have to be ruled out?

"Well, aren't you going to do anything? Anything at all?"

Paul stood up. "Thanks for the breakfast. I feel better." He took three long strides to the swinging door, pushed it open, and went through. He heard Laura say something as it swung shut, but he didn't go back to find out what it was.

He went to the stairway closet and worked Dunlap's report out of his overcoat pocket. There were four or five pages of it, inexpertly typed with double spaces. Paul stuffed it into the side pocket of his trousers and went upstairs. He stopped at the guest-room door and listened for a moment without shame before he knocked.

"Yeah, come on in," Stu called.

He was lying, still in his pajamas, on top of the sheet, reading a comic book. Paul thought his face was flushed. His pajamas were too tight, and he put his comic book down so that he could try to pull the edges together. He was wearing his new watch.

"You ought to be under the sheet," Paul said. "Didn't Robert's mother tell you that? You look feverish."

"Bob's mother took my temperature before they left. It ain't much." He pushed his legs down under the sheet obediently. "I wouldn't even be staying in bed like this, only she said to."

"She usually knows best about things of this kind."

"She said Laura was supposed to bring my lunch up to me, but I think I feel good enough to get dressed and go downstairs for it. Don't you think that would be okay?"

"No, I think you'd better stay right here, if that's what Robert's mother said." Paul sat down on the bed almost on Stu's feet. "It's no wonder you have a cold, out there in the grove like that last night, half dressed."

Stu looked frightened. "Gee whiz, Mr. Hamilton, we just . . ."

"What were you doing with your clothes off, Stu?"

"How did you find out? . . ." Stu pulled the sheet up to cover more of him, as if for protection. "I get in nothing but trouble. Bob made me tell him what you and me talked about yesterday, Mr. Hamilton. Well, gee whiz, I couldn't help it."

"Everything we talked about?"

"Pretty near. See, he was dragging my clothes off me, like my sheepskin and my sweater and everything, and I was about to freeze, and I knew I was gonna get pneumonia or something, so I just . . ." He looked down at his comic book, which was lying face down on the sheet. "I always was a big blabbermouth."

"Did Robert threaten to kill you, Stu?" Paul said it quietly, but it seemed to him to echo about the room as if he had shouted it.

"Huh? Oh, that was just part of the game . You know? He was gonna let me freeze to death and then put me back to bed and like that. He got six points for that one. You know, the game I was telling you about before."

"I see." Paul stood up. "Be sure you stay under that sheet. I'll be in to see you later."

Paul crossed the hall to the master bedroom and went in, closing the door firmly and wishing there were a way to lock it. He went into the study, sat down at his desk, and pulled Dunlap's report out of his pocket. He put it on the desk, face down, and sat for a long time looking down at the reverse side of the last page. He was sorry he had stopped in to see Stu. It hadn't done either of them any good. He wondered if Elaine had taken Robert away for the day because she was still afraid that he, Paul, meant the boy harm. The thought brought his tic back lightly. He snatched the report up angrily and began reading it.

It said, in more formal language, much the same thing Al Dunlap had said out in the back yard. It was a little more fully documented; that was the principal difference. A little more straightforward, a little harder to dismiss. Even though he had heard it all before, Paul felt the same sense of shock after reading it. He read it through again but found it just as hard to take the second time as the first.

There was a knock at the bedroom door. He stuffed the report into the desk's center drawer and called, "Come in."

Laura crept into the bedroom and moved halfway across it toward the study door. "I just gave Mr. Stuart his lunch, Mr. Hamilton. You want me to bring you something up here?"

"No, thanks, Laura."

"Well, then . . . will you want something downstairs later on?"

"I don't think so, no. If I get hungry later, I'll fix myself a turkey sandwich or something. Is there still some turkey left?"

"Yes, sir, plenty. Mr. Hamilton?"

"Yes?"

"I think Mr. Stuart's been crying."

"What!"

"Well, you know how your eyes get to looking after you've been crying. And he was kind of talking through his nose and everything."

"I'll go in and see him in a few minutes."

"Yes, sir."

After she had gone away, Paul took the report out of the desk drawer and read it once more. It had not improved in any way; it still said the same dreadful things. Paul folded it carefully and put it in the side pocket of his trousers. He stood for a moment, looking through the study door at the closed bedroom door, his face feeling grim. Then he went across the hall to Stu's door and knocked. He went in without waiting for Stu's permission.

Stu's tray was on the dresser across the room, untouched. He wasn't reading a comic book now, but just sitting there in his bed, doing nothing. Laura was right. He looked as if he had been crying.

Paul sat on the bed beside him and said, making his voice as gentle as he could, "Stu, why didn't you tell me the truth? Why did you lie to me?"

"Lie, Mr. Hamilton? What about?"

"About everything, Stu. The game, Johnny Spence, all of it. Why did you do that?"

Stu took a very deep breath that shuddered at the top. He said, "Mr. Hamilton, I want to go back to the Academy. I don't want to stay here anymore."

Chapter 21

ELAINE AND ROBERT came home just as dusk was turning to darkness. They had taken a long drive, Elaine said, had lunch at a sweet little place just miles and miles out on the Island, and then driven slowly back. "Such a shame Stuart wasn't able to come with us. It was lovely. The highways are all clear now, of course, but everything else is still covered with snow. We kept feeling so sorry for Stuart, cooped up here, all alone."

"Well, of course," Robert said, "he wasn't *quite* all alone, was he?"

"He wants to leave," Paul said flatly.

Elaine said, "What!"

"He wants to get out of this place and go back to the Academy."

"Why, I never head of such a thing!"

Robert said, "I'll talk to him. It'll be all right; don't worry. I'll talk to him."

It seemed an eternity before dinner was served. Paul wanted to stay away from them, from all of them, and there was no place for him to go. He had worn his old brown tweed suit, primarily because the jacket fitted loosely, so that there was plenty of room for Dunlap's report in the inside pocket. He kept wandering about the house, dodging the others, pressing his right elbow against his chest to make sure the report was still in his pocket. In the end, he retreated to the library and waited there, much as he despised the place, until dinner was announced.

Stu came down to dinner, still a little flushed and unable to look any of them in the eye. Elaine and Robert kept a light patter of talk going, but Paul didn't listen; he couldn't keep his eyes off Stu, and he couldn't get his mind off the thing in his jacket pocket. He realized only when he found both Elaine and Robert looking at him questioningly that somebody had spoken to him. "I'm sorry," he said. "Wool gathering."

Elaine said, "Robert wanted to know if you're all packed and ready for an early start for Vermont in the morning."

Vermont? "Oh. Are we still planning to go up to Vermont?" He had forgotten all about it since reading Elaine's note. It seemed absurd, after all that had happened, still to be planning to go skiing.

"Well, aren't we?"

"Of course, we are," Robert said. "Why shouldn't we? Oh, incidentally, Stu's changed his mind about going back to the Academy. Haven't you, Stu?"

Stu looked down at his plate. "Yeah, I changed my mind."

"So, why shouldn't we go?"

"All right," Paul said slowly. "All right, I'll pack after dinner. I don't know what kind of shape my skis are in. I'll have to take a look at them before I go to bed."

It was only an evasion, of course, what he had said. He felt quite sure that nobody was going to Vermont tomorrow. Whatever was going to happen had to happen tonight. And once it had happened, tomorrow was knocked into a cocked hat. Tomorrow and a lot of tomorrows after it. Elaine was looking at him as if she knew that he had no intention of going to Vermont.

Suddenly he had had as much dinner as he could eat or pretend to eat or even continue in the vicinity of without danger of a serious attack of nausea. He pushed his chair back and said, "I hope you'll excuse me. I have several things to do yet tonight, and I want to get to bed early, you know."

Elaine was still looking at him in that same way. "Are you all right?" He wondered how many times she had asked him that during the past two years. It wasn't the same this time. "You don't look very well at all."

Paul noticed that Robert was also eyeing him with what he might have taken for concern if he hadn't known better. "Oh, I'll be all right for tomorrow," he said. "There's nothing wrong with me. I feel a little tired, maybe, but that's all."

He was conscious of Robert's eyes on him as he left, almost a physical sensation, like a prickling between his shoulderblades. Laura was standing in the hallway just outside the dining room. She crooked a finger at him. Even though he was annoyed at being involved in an intrigue with Laura, he moved close enough to her to hear her whisper, "I have something else I have to tell you."

"Oh, for God's sake!"

"Sh! Can you come back to the kitchen after everybody's settled down in the living room or somewhere? I'v just got to tell you this, Mr. Hamilton."

"All right," Paul said. "I'm going outside, anyway." He had, just at that moment, decided that he had to get out of the place; it was stifling him. "I'll come back in by the kitchen door."

"Okay."

Although it had been his practice for two years to explain all his comings and goings to Elaine, he decided to forget it this time. As quietly as he could, not proud of the sneakiness of it, he got into his galoshes and overcoat. To avoid passing the dining-room opening, he went through the living room into the library and outside through the library's door. He walked back toward the grove, trying not to think about anything. He had the feeling that if he could just blank his mind out altogether while the cold, clean air was refreshing his body, he might, when he put it back to work, be able to think of some way to deal with the things that must be dealt with.

He walked back to where the grove started, turned to his right, and waded through the snow as far as the garage. He noticed that Laura's footprints were there, as she had said they would be, from the garage over to the grove and back. He walked the length of the driveway, out to the street, and looked up and down it without curiosity. It was empty. He went back up the driveway, slipping as badly as Al Dunlap had done, and around to the kitchen door. He opened it and went inside.

Laura turned away from the sink and came over to him with her stealthy walk, which was no longer as funny as he had thought it yesterday. "I think they all went upstairs," she said. "As close as I could tell from out here, that's where they all went."

"What was it you wanted to say to me?" Paul asked her.

"I don't expect you're going to like it."

Paul made a wry smile. "This has been my day for facing things I don't like. Go ahead."

"Well, I went in Mr. Robert's room again when you all first sat down to dinner this evening. I know you don't think I ought to, Mr. Hamilton, but . . ."

"It's all right," Paul said quietly. "I don't mind."

"I read some more in his diary."

"What did it say?"

"Well, Mr. Hamilton, it just keeps on saying he's going to kill you. I didn't find a word in there about any stupid games or any of that; just that he's got a plan how to kill you. Tomorrow, while you're out there at that place skiing. Belt you over the head with something and then push you on down a cliff or whatever's handy. I'm telling you, honest, Mr. Hamilton, that's what it says, and it sure don't sound like any little old game to me."

Paul nodded. "I agree with you."

Laura looked comically astonished. "You do!"

"I'm afraid I do. That was a detective you saw me talking to this morning. He convinced me of a lot of things."

"So, what are you going to do?" There was something ugly about her eagerness. "Are you going to call the police?"

"Is he up in his room now?"

"I think so."

"I'm going to go up and see him." There simply wasn't any more time. There wasn't any more time at all. "It's no good waiting until I have a plan," he said, talking to himself rather than Laura. "What I have to do is just start something and then go wherever it takes me."

Laura's face was flushed now, not a great improvement over her customary pallor. "I'm pretty sure he went upstairs," she said. "He must be in his room."

Paul slipped out of his overcoat and handed it to Laura. While he was struggling to get out of his galoshes, he said, "Put these things away for me, please."

"You want me to go up with you, Mr. Hamilton? I won't be scared of him with you there, and maybe I could——"

"No! You stay right here where you are. I don't want him to find out you've been talking to me."

"Oh!" The color drained quickly out of Laura's face. "All right. Yes. I'll stay right here." She put Paul's coat down on the kitchen table. "I hope you give it to him good, though."

Paul made his way quietly but without conscious stealth up to the second floor. He felt thoroughly committed and quite calm. The tic had left his mouth. He stopped for a moment and listened at Robert's door, but there was nothing to hear. Suddenly he twisted the knob and pushed the door with unnecessary violence, so that it crashed against the wall. Robert had been sitting at his desk, reading from the looseleaf notebook. He half stood at the sound of Paul's entrance, pulled open the center drawer of his desk, and scrabbling uncharacteristically, tried to get the book into it.

"I'll have a look at that thing," Paul said.

Robert's only answer was a sort of growl from somewhere deep inside him. It sounded uncivilized enough for killing.

Paul crossed the room in four long strides. Insanely, he counted them. With his right hand he seized Robert's shoulder—not just the jacket, but the shoulder as well—and with his left scooped up the notebook, which Robert had never succeeded in getting wholly into the drawer.

"Take your hands off me," Robert said softly.

"Shut up."

Spreading the book open on the desk, Paul leaned a little away from Robert, stooping over the desk, and with his free left hand riffled the pages until he came to the final entry. He read:

December 27:
Everything arranged for sad passing of stepfather. As good as J. S. Maybe too much like J. S. Only trouble. But can't argue with success.
Skiing tomorrow. Didn't think at first he'd agree to go. How stupid can you get? Shouldn't be a crowd on a weekday. Trick is to stay close behind until nobody watching and then bash him with ski pole. Not quite as easy as J. S., but easy enough. Then stage bad fall. Down steep slope if lucky enough to have one handy. Have to gamble a little. Who'd dream of accusing me, anyway?
Looking forward to it. Been a long wait. Feel ready. Nerves excellent.

Paul straightened and looked at Robert, almost smiling. "How are your nerves now?"

Robert made an odd twisting movement, completely without warning, and pulled free. Paul had known that Robert possessed a certain animal agility, but the sheer strength involved in the maneuver startled him. He saw Robert throw a quick sidewise glance at the bed where his new rifle lay, and he had his own long legs to thank for getting him there first. He planted a knee on the rifle and twisted back, reaching for Robert. With insulting ease, Robert spun away from him and disappeared into the hallway.

Paul paused long enough to gather up Robert's diary and stuff it into one of the wide side pockets of his jacket before following the boy out into the hall. By this time Robert was nowhere to be seen, but Paul heard the dull thump of his running steps on the carpeted stairway. He reached the top of the stairs just in time to see Robert clear the bottom step, and making a wide turn, head into the living room. Paul was halfway to the bottom himself before he realized that he was taking the steps two at a time with no regard for the bones he had been thinking of as brittle only yesterday. He reached the bottom in time to see Robert disappear into the library, slamming the door behind him.

Paul crossed the living room and opened the library door with another crash. Robert was standing in a half-lounging attitude, wonderfully relaxed, at the opposite end of the room, between the gun case and the outside door. The glass door of the gun case was open. Robert was holding a rifle at hip level.

"Well," Robert said casually, "we're about the same size now, wouldn't you say? Or maybe I'm a little bigger." He wasn't even breathing hard.

Without answering, Paul took a step into the room.

Robert shook his head. "I wouldn't if I were you. This thing is loaded." He waggled the rifle. "They're always loaded, all of them, all the time, as I once told you. Did you bring the diary with you, or is it still up in my room?"

Paul said, "You'd never be able to make it look like an accident if you pulled that trigger now."

"I'll think of something if I have to," Robert said placidly. "I'm very clever."

Paul moved forward another step.

"Maybe you think I'll miss," Robert said. He pointed. "See that book on the top shelf? Red one, third from the end? See the circle at the bottom for the publisher's name? Watch." He lifted the rifle to his shoulder, sighted with extravagant carelessness, and fired. The noise startled Paul, even though he had been warned. A small hole appeared almost at the exact center of the circle Robert had pointed out.

Robert worked the reloading mechanism, making a deadly sound in the stillness that followed the shot. "If you want to do something stupid," he said mildly, "go ahead. The next little hole I make will be right in the middle of your forehead." He tipped a corner of his mouth up. "And don't worry about me. I'll get out of it, all right."

He moved cautiously, as though actually stalking, over toward the door that opened onto the lawn outside. Paul could think of nothing to say, and he saw no profit in moving.

"Robert?" It was Elaine's voice from the hall or perhaps the stairway. "Robert, where are you?"

"Mother!" Robert said. He reached behind him and opened the door. "I'm going to give you an even chance," he said. "That's the way I like to do things. That's the way my father liked to do things. I'm going out into the grove. You take one of those rifles —they're all loaded—"—he nodded backward toward the gun case—"and you come out after me if you've got the guts. Take a shotgun if you want." He smiled, pleased with himself. "Big-game hunting on darkest Long Island." He slipped through the door and closed it softly.

"Robert?" Elaine called.

Paul crossed to the door and peered out through the glass panel. It was a dark night, but he could see Robert silhouetted against the snow, running toward the grove, bent forward as though expecting to be fired upon.

"Robert?" As Paul turned, Elaine appeared in the doorway. "What's going on, Paul? Where's Robert? I thought I heard a shot."

Paul nodded. "You sure did."

"Well, what happened?"

"He shot a hole in that book." Paul pointed. "That was to convince me he could hit what he aimed at. The next one was to make a hole in the center of my forehead. He'd have done it, too, if I hadn't let him get away."

"Paul, what in heaven's name are you talking about?"

"I blame myself," Paul told her. "I should have spoken to you the night he got here. Elaine—I'm sorry, Elaine—Robert killed a boy up at Hastings."

The expression drained completely out of Elaine's face, leaving it artificial-looking. "That's not true!"

Paul nodded sadly. "It's true, all right."

"That's a . . . that's a dreadful thing to say! I think you must be out of your mind."

"All right. He's out there in the grove now with one of his father's old rifles. He's invited me to come out after him. Shall I go? If I'm just making all this up out of my addled head, then I'll be perfectly safe, won't I?"

"I won't listen to you!"

Paul took a step or two toward her and was grieved to see her move just a little back toward the door. "All right," he said, "here." He drew Al Dunlap's report out of his inside jacket pocket and tossed it onto the desk near her. "That's the report of a detective I hired to check on the death of a kid named Johnny Spence up at Hastings last month. And here." He worried Robert's diary out of his side pocket and tossed it onto the desk near Dunlap's report. "That's Robert's diary. It has a very dramatic ending. All about how he plans to kill me tomorrow at that damn ski place. Read them, Elaine. Just read them and then decide who is out of whose mind."

Elaine moved toward the desk. She seemed to be hypnotized by the sight of Robert's diary.

"The report first, I think," Paul said, but as she picked up the notebook, "All right then, the diary; I don't care."

She lowered herself into the leather chair near the desk and opened the book. Paul watched her until he was sure that she was thoroughly engrossed, and then, moving back silently, he reached into the gun case and selected a rifle at random. It was heavy and unwieldy, but he hadn't expected a gun to feel natural in his hands. Elaine didn't look up. He went to the door, opened it quietly, stepped outside, and made his way cautiously down the two slippery steps, sharply conscious of the light in the room behind him.

Chapter 22

IT SEEMED TO Paul that the very silence had a waiting quality. Ordinary nocturnal restlessness and rustlings were suspended in awed anticipation. The night was windless and moonless. Stars were sparse and indecently remote. The snow was white only insofar as it made contrast with the world of less white things. It seemed an extraordinarily alert night.

Once he had stepped out of the rectangle of light he had made by opening the door, Paul doubted that he could be seen from the grove. He stayed where he was at the foot of the steps and a little to their left, shivering, his mouth twitching. He had no plan. Again, he thought, he had been caught with his plans down. It didn't seem very funny. There was little value in planning, anyway. Any workable plan would depend upon Robert, presupposing his behavior, a preposterous thing to presuppose.

With a little sigh for the rashness of it, Paul bent double and began to run for the grove, zigzagging in a way that he knew must look insane to anybody who was not thinking of him as a target. The gun seemed to drag at his arm; he thought he must have chosen the heaviest one in the case. He wondered if he would be able to use it. Peaceful men used guns in time of war, but, of course, this wasn't a real war. If it were, somebody else would be carrying the gun and running the zigzag pattern. Men his age would be at home making money. He recognized this kind of thinking as irrational, or at least idle, which was just as bad.

He reached the grove without being shot at. Plunging into the shadow of the nearest tree, he was lashed across the face at once by something with thorns on it. He stopped short, realizing that the safety of the grove was a comparative thing. If he kept on running he was almost certain to bash in his head against a tree or, at best, to advertise his whereabouts by his thrashing about. For all he knew, Robert might at this moment be standing a matter of inches away.

"All right," Robert called. He was not nearby, at least; he was a comforting distance away, but in what direction, Paul was unable to determine very definitely from the sound. A little to the south, perhaps, and certainly deep into the darkness. "All right, I let you get to the grove. I could have knocked you off anytime, but I don't shoot sitting ducks. I see you brought a gun with you."

Paul was not foolish enough to answer him. He put the rifle to his shoulder, feeling a good deal more ridiculous than dangerous.

"I'll give you the first shot," Robert called. "The trick is to aim at the sound of my voice. Of course, once you fire, I have something better to aim at." He laughed lightly, with depressing confidence. "I know every tree in this grove and every bush and every rock. And I know how to hunt in the dark. My father taught me that. Go ahead and fire."

Paul found that he could not. He had located Robert as accurately as he was ever going to from the sound of his voice, and he had the gun pointed in what he felt to be the right direction, but he could not pull the trigger. What he was afraid of was not that he might miss Robert, but that he might hit him. He took the rifle down from his shoulder, stooped, and laid it as quietly as he could on the ground beside him. It was only going to hamper him if he went on carrying it.

He had to move; that much was certain. Robert must know pretty definitely at what point he had entered the grove, and what Robert had meant by knowing how to hunt in the dark, Paul felt sure, was that he could aim by sound and from memory as well as by sight. It did not occur to Paul to doubt Robert's ability; he had seen him exhibit too many talents too often. He faced left and extended his arms before him, feeling for obstructions. Finding none, he took a cautious step forward. Still there was nothing in his way. He took another step, and another, and then, with a sharpness that made his ears twitch, a twig snapped under his foot.

There was an answering crack, hardly louder than the sound the twig had made. Off to his right and perhaps fifty yards away, he saw a shockingly bright spurt of light, yellowish-red and gone at once, leaving a streak on his retina. He didn't hear the bullet. Or feel it. He smiled grimly.

He had to move again, he knew, and without delay. He took a quick sidestep to his right and three long reckless strides forward, coming up sharply but silently against the bole of a large tree, his outstretched arms encircling it. A hickory, from the feel, he thought pointlessly. It was icy to the touch. It made him shiver.

"Robert!"

It was Elaine's voice, and Paul forgot his own danger, not so much heroically as absentmindedly. He took a careless step back the way he had come, and through the space between the trunks of two thick trees he could see Elaine, sharply and very beautifully silhouetted in the light from the open library door.

"Robert! Is that you shooting?"

"Elaine, get back!" Paul shouted. He thought that Robert must surely be insane, and although he didn't know that he would shoot at his own mother, he also didn't know that he would not. "For God's sake, get back inside the house and shut the door!"

The rifle cracked again, from behind Paul this time. The bullet ricocheted off something and whined past him, very near. At least that meant that Robert was shooting at him and not at Elaine. It was a terrible thing to think that a boy might shoot his own mother, but Paul found that he had grown accustomed to thinking terrible things about Robert.

"Paul, are you all right?"

At least she had thought about it. "Yes. Elaine, please do as I say! Shut the door. Go inside and shut the door. You're right in the light. Or come outside if you have to, but shut the door. There's no telling what he may do. Please!"

He heard another of Robert's light, pleased laughs and then the report of his rifle. There was no whining sound this time, and Paul waited, holding his breath, for the bullet to enter his flesh. He remembered only after seconds had passed that you didn't have to wait for a bullet to strike. Either it did or it didn't, right then. This one had not.

The light from the open library door had disappeared. "If you're outside, Elaine," Paul shouted, "stay where you are. I can't see you from here, and I don't believe he can, either. Stay close to the house. Don't try to come down here."

The rifle cracked again and the bullet screamed. He heard a slapping noise just to his right, very near. The sound a bullet made going into a tree, he supposed. Thinking of what Elaine must be going through, he felt a surge of hatred for Robert, in his body just as much as in his mind. It was a prickly feeling in his chest. It seemed to step everything up. It made him feel strong, invincible.

"Robert," he called, "you've painted yourself into a corner; do you know that? If you kill me the police will get you, and if you don't, then I'll get you and give you to the police. Any way it comes out, you lose."

The rifle sounded again. This time, since he had turned to face Robert, the flash blinded him and he imagined he could feel the breeze made by the passing bullet.

"You're not even aiming in the right direction," he shouted. "Is that the best your father taught you? I think I could do better myself, if I wanted to try."

There was a violent thrashing sound from the direction of the shooting.

Paul grinned. "What's the matter now?" The grin felt satanic on his face; it felt good. "Did you come across a bush you hadn't met before?"

After more of the thrashing, the rifle cracked again. From what Paul could see of the lightninglike spurt of flame, Robert had fired far to the left.

Paul laughed aloud. "That was closer, but you're still a mile off."

"Dirty bastard! Dirty bastard!"

It had not been Robert's voice, Paul realized with a shock. His first thought was of Elaine, but it hadn't been her voice, either, and, in any case, in any extremity, she would never have said such a thing. He began pushing his way blindly, caroming off trees, clutched at by thorny bushes, toward the sound of thrashing, which continued.

"Stu!" he shouted. "Stu, get away! Get back!"

"Mr. Hamilton!" Stu's voice, in distress, sounded even less mature than normally. "I think I got him, but hurry up."

"All right. Keep on making some kind of noise, though. I can't see you."

The noise Stu chose to make was, "Dirty bastard, dirty bastard, dirty bastard." He made it a sort of incantation, which, quite devoid of meaning after a few repetitions, served as a very workable beacon.

"Are you standing up or lying on the ground, Stu?"

"On the ground," Stu said. His voice was quite near now. "I got him by the legs. I tackled him pretty good. He's still got the gun, though."

As if to bear Stu out, there was a sharp report and an unbearably bright flash of light close at hand. Paul realized with the bullet's own speed that Robert had missed again. He dived forward to a spot just behind where the flash had appeared and landed on something that squirmed. There was a gruff sound which was mostly the expulsion of air. Paul hoped that it was Robert and not Stu he had knocked the breath out of.

"Get the gun, Mr. Hamilton," Stu said urgently. "The two of us can lick him easy if you can get the gun."

Paul felt along the back up to the shoulders and outward along both arms. He found the rifle clutched in Robert's right hand and wrenched it away before Robert had a chance to resist seriously.

"All right," Robert said quietly, although with a suggestion of breathlessness, "get off me, for Christ's sake, will you?"

Paul took Robert's right wrist in one of his big hands and with pure strength slowly bent the arm double and tucked it down against the back, the hand up near the shoulderblades. It was what the wrestling announcers on television called a hammerlock, he believed, and the application of it to Robert felt very satisfactory.

Robert squirmed, trying to shake Paul off. "You're hurting my shoulder."

"Fine," Paul said. "Stand up. Get up on your feet."

"Let go of my arm and I will."

"You're not going to talk me out of a thing," Paul told him. "Get up."

There was a rustling sound behind him, and Paul, now on one knee, whirled about, forcing a grunt of pain from Robert, who was trying to get his feet under him. A shadowy shape in the darkness only a few yards away proved to be Elaine.

"Robert?"

Robert, his feet now firmly beneath him, made a strong lunge forward, but Paul's grip on his wrist held. Brought up short, as though at the end of a leash, he made a startlingly shrill screaming sound. "My shoulder!"

Paul said, "Then hold still."

"Oh, Robert!" Elaine took a hesitant step toward them. "Robert, Robert!"

"Mother, he's hurting me. Make him stop."

"I'm afraid I am hurting him, just a little," Paul told Elaine reasonably, "but it can't be helped."

"I think he's broken my shoulder."

"I've done nothing of the sort, but I will if you try to get away again. Are you all right, Stu?"

Stu, struggling to his feet only now, made a fat grunting noise and then said, "I guess so. He kicked me in the stomach when I tackled him, but it don't hurt so much now. I was up in my room and I heard a gun go off or something. I thought I better see what was up."

"A good thing you did, too," Paul said quietly.

"You know, he tried to *shoot* me?"

Paul grinned, knowing that no one could see it in the darkness. "That makes two of us."

"Robert," Elaine said, "how could you? What *is* it, Robert? What's the matter?"

Robert said, "Tell him to take his hands off me."

Paul tightened his grip on Robert's wrist. "Let's get back to the house."

"He was going to kill you, Mr. Hamilton," Stu said, hardly believing his own words. "Tomorrow. He told me. Out there while you were skiing, he was going to. I think he's nuts."

"Don't say that, Stuart!" Elaine took a step toward Stu. "That's a terrible thing to say!"

"Excuse me," Stu said to her politely. "And you know what, Mr. Hamilton? He did kill Johnny Spence. I mean for real, not just in the game."

"It might have saved some trouble if you'd told me that yesterday, Stu," Paul said quietly.

"But I didn't know! All the guys at the Academy thought Johnny just moved out west. I mean, that's what they told us. Honest, Mr. Hamilton. Only Bob got to bragging about Johnny tonight when he was talking about killing you. And, you know what I think? I think he's gonna kill me, too! On account of I know too much. Boy, do I ever know too much!"

"He isn't going to kill anybody," Paul said. "Let's get back into the house." He urged Robert forward. "The sooner we get this over with, the better."

He pushed Robert ahead of him through the grove. He could hear Elaine and Stu following. Robert peered back over his left shoulder, back past Paul, and said, "Mother, if I promise not to run away, will you make him stop hurting me?"

Elaine said, "Paul?"

Paul shook his head uselessly in the darkness. "I'm sorry. His promises don't mean a thing. If I let him go, he'll get away again. We can't afford to keep on giving him chances. He might have better luck the next time. Besides, I'm not hurting him that much. I forgot to bring the rifle."

"I got it, Mr. Hamilton," Stu said. "I must have bumped into a tree or something. My arm's beginning to hurt like anything."

"You're lucky you didn't get shot," Paul told him. "I think I have to thank you for saving my life."

"Oh, Paul!" Elaine said. "He wouldn't have shot you! I know how it looks, but——"

"Did you read that stuff I gave you?" Paul interrupted.

"Yes, the last part of the diary. I was finishing the report when I heard the gun go off."

"He'd have killed me, all right, if he could have found me."

"In spades," Robert growled.

"Now, Robert," Elaine said in the baby-admonishing voice she sometimes used so foolishly with Robert. "Now, Robert, you know perfectly well you're just showing off. Shooting off the gun and causing a lot of excitement is one thing, but——"

"Oh, Mother, shut up, will you?"

There was a long silence, which Paul thought he would be a fool to break.

At last Elaine said softly, "You really were shooting at him, weren't you, Robert?"

"Look," Robert said, "whose side are you going to be on, his or mine? Of course, I was shooting at him, and if I'd hit him we could make it look like an accident, and everything would be all right. The way things have turned out now, it's all going to be up to you. It's going to have to be your word against his. I can handle Stu. It'll be just your word against his."

"And you killed the Spence boy, didn't you?"

"What's that got to do with this?"

"You really intended to hit Paul, didn't you?"

"What's the matter with you, anyway? Of course I intended to hit him. Right between the God damn eyes. Try not to be stupid, Mother, will you?"

Elaine had nothing more to say. They had left the grove—escaped from it, Paul thought—and were moving up toward the house, silently now except for the squeak of their steps on the dry snow. At the last moment, Stu ran ahead and opened the library door for them, letting out a dazzling shaft of light.

As he pushed Robert past Stu and up the steps, Paul glanced down idly and then took a closer look at Stu. From just below the shoulder down to the wrist of his right arm, the sleeve was stained crimson. The blood ran down in several small rivulets along the back of his hand and discolored the barrel of the rifle he was carrying.

"Elaine," Paul said, thinking it might be good for both of them, "will you take a look at Stu's arm?"

Stu waited for Elaine to pass through the doorway and then looked down at the arm himself. The abruptness with which his face turned white had, like everything else he did, an element of comedy in it. "Judas Priest!" he said. "I think I've been shot!"

"I'm afraid so," Paul told them all. "Come on over here; let me have a look."

"I'll take care of it," Elaine said. Her tone was so flat that Paul threw her a quick, inquiring glance. Her face had a set, negative look that it had never worn before to Paul's knowledge, an absence of expression that was an eloquent expression in itself. She was very pale in spite of the cold. They had all been out there without coats or hats or overshoes. Kneeling beside Stu, Elaine peeled back a shred of his torn sleeve. "It only grazed him, I think," she said, almost impersonally. "He's been bleeding quite a lot, but it seems to have stopped now."

"I'll call Dr. Strong," Paul said.

Elaine rose stiffly. "I'll call him. You hold Robert."

Robert looked startled. "Mother, he doesn't have to hold me. I've told you I won't run away. Why should I run away? It's only his word against yours. Tell him to let me go."

Elaine, seeming not to have heard Robert, went to the telephone on the desk.

"Mrs. Hamilton," Stu said, "it don't hurt so much now. I'd feel better if you'd call the cops first. I mean, that's more important." He looked up at Paul. "Don't you think that's more important?"

Elaine turned her stony look upon Stu and after a little pause said, "The police?"

"I can do it," Paul told her.

"No." She turned back and lifted the phone.

"Mother!" Robert screamed. His voice had gone shrill again. "What do you think you're doing?"

"Be quiet, Robert," was all she said. She dialed once and waited. "Operator, I want the police."

"Mother!"

Elaine faced Robert at last, and the stony expression melted. "I'm sorry, Robert. I'm so sorry."

"They have the best psychiatrists in the business," Paul said, remembering Al Dunlap. "None of that handcuff, bread-and-water, brutality business anymore. They'll help him; that's what their job is. That's what they're there for. I mean, they'll—"

Elaine turned her sad look on Paul. "There isn't any choice anyway, is there?"

"Mother!" The word was spoken in such an odd, broken voice that Paul leaned forward to look at Robert's face. It was twisted grotesquely out of shape.

"Oh," Elaine said into the telephone. "Is this the police?" She nodded. "Yes. I want you to come out to the Hamilton place on Shore Road; do you know where that is? Yes, the old Reagan place." She turned and smiled wanly at Robert. "There's been . . . I guess you'd say an attempted murder. And, we think, a real murder a while back. Yes, we're all right now. My husband has . . . has taken care of things. Yes, as soon as you can. Oh, if you could bring a doctor . . . Yes, somebody's been shot, you see. Dr. Strong is our family doctor. Thank you." She replaced the telephone carefully, as if not wanting to make a noise with it.

Robert said thickly, "But, Mother, they'll take me away." He bowed his head. The sobs were widely spaced, and each one shook him to his toes. They had a masculine, adult sound that was dreadful to hear. As far as Paul knew, it was the first time Robert had cried since Dr. Strong had paddled his newly born behind, if he had cried even then. He repeated with a bubbly sound, "They'll take me away!"

Elaine nodded. "I know, dear."